"This is where you belong, Tessie," he murmured against her willing lips. *"Here in my arms."*

Waves of pleasure swept over her as she leaned into him.

"You're my wife, Tessie," he whispered, nuzzling his chin in her hair. "This is where God intended you to be."

Tessa shifted in his arms as reality struck. Other than the two of them having a few good times as they'd worked on Katie's wedding, nothing had changed. Mike was still Mike the cop. Mike, the man who always put his work above all else in his life. The man who cared little about the time he spent away from his family or the danger he faced every day. Needing to free herself from his grasp, Tessa placed her hands on his chest and pushed away. "I may have belonged in your arms once, but not now. The only thing that has changed between us, Mike, is that we've grown older and probably each more set in our ways. While I don't like living alone, I've resigned myself to it, and I'm doing quite nicely. And yes, I'm sure God wanted us to be together, but apparently the only way you wanted us to be together was on your terms. Not His."

With a grunt of exasperation, Mike stood and gave his head a shake. "Maybe I'd better go."

Working hard at keeping her tears at bay, she turned her face away from him. "That's probably a very good idea."

Mike grabbed the remaining slice of pizza from his plate and, without looking back or saying another word, moved quickly through the house and out the front door. It slammed hard behind him, leaving Tessa brokenhearted and dreading her next meeting with him.

JOYCE LIVINGSTON has done many things in her life (in addition to being a wife, mother of six, and grandmother to oodles of grandkids, all of whom she loves dearly). From being a television broadcaster for eighteen years, to lecturing and teaching on quilting and sewing, to writing magazine articles on a variety of subjects. She's danced with Lawrence Welk, ice-skated with a chimpanzee, had bottles broken over her head by stuntmen, interviewed hundreds of celebrities and controversial figures, and many other interesting and unusual things. But now, when she isn't off traveling to wonderful and exotic places as a part-time tour escort, her days are spent sitting in front of her computer, creating stories. She feels her writing is a ministry and a calling from God, and she hopes Heartsong readers will be touched and uplifted by what she writes. Joyce loves to hear from her readers and invites you to visit her on the Internet at: www.joycelivingston.com

Books by Joyce Livingston

HEARTSONG PRESENTS

Don't miss out on any of our super romances. Write to us at the following address for information on our newest releases and club information.

Heartsong Presents Readers' Service
PO Box 721
Uhrichsville, OH 44683

Or visit www.heartsongpresents.com

Love
Worth Keeping

Joyce Livingston

Heartsong Presents

I dedicate this book to my wonderful children, their sweet spouses, and their families who stood with me through this very trying year as we faced the eminent death of my dear husband—their father and grandfather. I could never have made it through this time with you and your unselfish love: Dawn Lee, Don Jr. and Helen, Mark and Cat, Dari and Wally, Matthew and Sherry, Luke and Tammie. I love you all more than words can say. You are all a gift from God. Thank you, thank you, thank you.

And, as always, this book and any other book I may ever write, is dedicated to my precious husband and my greatest fan, Don Livingston. Don, you may be gone but my love for you will never die.

A note from the Author:
I love to hear from my readers! You may correspond with me by writing:

Joyce Livingston
Author Relations
PO Box 719
Uhrichsville, OH 44683

ISBN 1-59310-610-6

LOVE WORTH KEEPING

All scripture quotations are taken from the King James Version of the Bible.

All of the characters and events in this book are fictitious. Any resemblance to actual persons, living or dead, or to actual events is purely coincidental.

Our mission is to publish and distribute inspirational products offering exceptional value and biblical encouragement to the masses.

PRINTED IN THE U.S.A.

one

"A Christmas wedding?" Tessa Garrett stared at her daughter in wide-eyed amazement then shook her head disapprovingly. "Impossible. Christmas is only two weeks away!"

"Mom, Jim and I have already decided we're not going to wait until spring when I graduate from college. We want to get married on Christmas Day, like you and Daddy did. I've already called about the church and. . ." Katie's eyes lit up as she chattered on, apparently oblivious to her mother's bewildered response.

Tessa held up her hands in defeat and heaved a sigh, knowing from experience once Katie's mind was made up there was little use trying to argue with her. That child was just like her father—strong-willed and stubborn. This was not at all what she'd wanted for her precious daughter. She'd envisioned a spring wedding, maybe held in the arboretum, with bridesmaids in pastel gowns, winding matching ribbons around a maypole, and—

"Earth to Mother," Katie chimed in a playful manner as she waved her hands before Tessa's face. "Yoo-hoo!"

Tessa offered a weak smile and attempted to keep disappointment from tainting her voice. "Well, I suppose I should be grateful you've decided to get married, rather than continue to live together, like you two have done for the past few months. Given the two choices, I'd opt for a wedding any day."

Katie's eyes widened. "What? You're not going to try to convince me to wait?"

5

Tessa eyed her beautiful daughter, her heart filled with love for this child who had so quickly grown into a woman. "It sounds like an impossible task but. . ." She swallowed hard, trying to avoid the argument she knew was inevitable if she didn't agree to this sudden wedding. Knowing how impulsive Katie could be, her headstrong daughter might even elope, and she'd miss being a part of the most important day in her child's life. "I—ah—I guess Christmas Day is as good as any. If you're certain you want to go through with this—"

"Yes, I do want to!" Katie threw her arms about her mother's neck and kissed her cheek repeatedly, her face shining with joy. "Oh, Mom, I love you. I told Jim you'd see it our way. This is so exciting! I'm going to be married. In just two weeks!"

"Look," Tessa began as she glanced around the busy restaurant, her voice now soft and pleading, knowing full well her determined daughter was not one to be reckoned with under the best of circumstances. "I'm happy you've decided to tie the knot. You know I've never liked the idea of you and Jim living together. It's just something we Christians don't do."

Katie muffled a giggle as she stole a quick glance at her fiancé of six months who was sitting silently beside her, their chairs pulled close together at the small, round table. Jim appeared extremely nervous about the conversation going on between the two women. "*We* Christians? I know of a number—"

"Mind your tongue, Katie Garrett. What others do, Christians or not, is not relevant; it's what God's Word says that counts. You know He would never approve of such a thing."

"Yes, I know." Katie snickered then asked, "So? I guess that means you're okay with our Christmas wedding?"

Tessa leaned back in her chair and crossed her arms over her chest, an eyebrow lifted in question. "As if what I said would make any difference?"

Katie grinned. "Well—"

"I rest my case." Tessa shook her head as a slow smile crept across her face. "Well, is it to be a Christmas Eve or a Christmas Day wedding?"

"Jim wanted it to be Christmas Eve. I wanted Christmas Day, early evening."

"So, which is it?"

Jim, who'd uttered barely a word until now, slipped an arm about Katie's shoulders and pulled her close. "Christmas Day."

The three laughed.

Tessa's mood sobered. "What about premarital counseling? I know Pastor McIntosh requires it of all the couples he marries."

"We've already met with him, Mom. He really laid it on the line for both of us. I've decided it's time for me to get my life back together. I've been away from the Lord way too long."

"I've accepted Christ as my Savior. Katie and I are both really excited about our relationship with God. I have a lot to learn, and Katie said she does, too. We're going to start attending the Young Married Class at Seaside Community Church. Oh, and Katie forgot to mention that I've moved out of the condo temporarily. One of my single coworkers offered to let me stay with him until after our wedding."

Tessa wanted to shout hallelujah. She'd been praying for Katie for so long, and God had answered her prayer. She reached across the table and cupped her soon-to-be son-in-law's hand. "You have no idea how happy this makes me."

Katie leaned her head onto Jim's shoulder affectionately. "I knew you'd be happy about it, Mom. I probably should have told you after we met with Pastor McIntosh, but I wanted Jim to be here when I told you."

"So Christmas Day it is. But Christmas, Katie? Couldn't

you have at least made it New Year's Day? Two weeks to plan and prepare for a wedding, even a small wedding, isn't nearly enough time." Tessa pulled a little calendar from the pocket in her checkbook and began to scan the dates in December.

"Enough time for what?" Katie's good-looking father asked as he removed his coat, kissed the younger woman on the forehead, and then dropped into a chair beside Tessa. "Sorry I'm late."

Tessa felt her smile disappear and her face blanch. She avoided the man's eyes and stared at her daughter. "What is *he* doing here?" she asked, wishing he weren't yet suddenly feeling self-conscious. The ambivalence she felt toward Mike was infuriating, and his presence always made her behave irrationally.

"I," the man announced proudly as he tossed his coat onto a nearby empty chair, "was invited here to have lunch with my lovely daughter." With a tender smile and a nod, he gestured toward Katie, who was seated directly across the table, then shook hands with Jim. "And although I'm not sure why she'd want the two of us to be in the same place at the same time, considering how you feel about me, I'm glad she did."

Tessa answered by crossing her arms and tilting her chin. "You'll find out soon enough."

He rubbed his hands together vigorously as if in anticipation and focused his attention on his daughter. "What's up, kiddo?"

Katie's eyes sparkled as she latched onto her father's hand and gave it a squeeze. "Jim and I are getting married!"

His face brightened. "No more of this cohabitation stuff?"

Katie blushed. "Nope, we're tying the knot, as Mom says."

He let out a long sigh of relief. "Glad to hear it. I never did like that arrangement."

"You sound like Mom! You should also be glad to hear that

Jim is staying with a single coworker temporarily. Jim is a brand-new Christian, Daddy."

"You're right; I am happy to hear that—both parts. Congratulations, Jim. Glad to see you'll be starting out on the right foot to build a solid marriage."

Tessa waited until the waiter moved on before speaking her peace. "Yes, but I'm sure Jim won't follow Mike's example—"

Katie thumped her hand on the table. "Mom, please! Can't you two be in the same room for five minutes without sniping at one another?"

"I never said a word," her father interjected defensively. "Your mother started it, as usual."

Quickly shoving back her chair and rising to her feet, Katie wadded up her napkin and tossed it onto her plate. "Either you two call a cease-fire, or I'm leaving, and Jim and I will elope."

Tessa grabbed at her daughter's wrist. "Katie, you're making a scene. Please sit down," she urged quietly.

"Say you're sorry, Mother, or we're outta here." Her daughter waited, her accusing gaze fixed on Tessa's face.

She swallowed hard. "Okay. I—I'm sorry."

Katie sank slowly into her chair. "Don't tell *me*," she said with a nod toward her father. "Tell him."

"Katie, I—"

Her daughter narrowed her eyes and cocked her head, her expression serious. "Now, please, or we're history."

Tessa sucked in her breath and held it. If there was anything she hated to do when it came to the husband she'd separated herself from, it was to admit she'd been in the wrong—about anything. But apparently, this time, she had no choice. "Oh, all right," she said, her gaze still pinned on Katie. "I'm sorry, Mike."

"At least you could look at me when you apologize, Tessie," Mike remarked with a taunting smile in his voice. "I can't remember the last time I heard you apologize. For anything."

Tessa watched as Katie's finger flew into her father's face. "And now you need to tell Mom *you're* sorry! That remark was uncalled-for, Daddy."

"See?" Tessa snapped, no longer caring about those seated around them hearing their conversation. "That's what I knew I'd get from that man. Nothing but snide remarks." *Even though what he said is true,* she reluctantly admitted to herself, trying to recall her last sincere apology to Mike.

Katie rose slightly, bent toward the quarrelsome pair, and stuck her chin out defiantly, her hands braced on the table, a look of disgust etched across her face. "I can't believe this. You two are worse than a couple of kindergartners. Why can't you be like other divorced or separated parents and bury the hatchet somewhere other than in each other's heads? You've been apart for eight years now. It's about time the two of you grew up!"

Mike leaned back in his chair, linking his fingers over his chest with a look of contrition. "Oh, pumpkin, I'm sorry. Your mom seems to bring out the worst in me."

"In you?" Tessa retorted, her anger rising again. "What about what you do to me?"

Katie's fist hit the table. "Stop it! Now! I refuse to tolerate this childishness one second more!"

The entire restaurant grew silent as waiters and customers stared in their direction. Jim, his face now a deep crimson, raised his water glass and took a long drink. Tessa slid down in her chair, wishing she'd kept her voice down to a whisper. "I'm sorry, Katie. I never meant to upset you."

Mike gave Tessa a pensive glance before turning his attention back to Katie. "I'm sorry, too, pumpkin."

"Good. Thank you," Katie said as she sat down. "Now that we've all settled down and will hopefully stay that way," she added softly, eyeing first one parent and then the other, "do you want to hear about our wedding plans?"

Each gave her a sheepish nod.

Donning a fresh smile, Katie took Jim's hand, her enthusiasm obviously rekindled. "Jim and I thought—"

"First," Tessa interrupted, still rankled at having to share this moment with her estranged husband, "I just want to say that this incident wouldn't have happened if you'd told me he was invited today. Although I wasn't expecting him, your father's late arrival was a vivid reminder—"

"Mother! Let it rest! It's not important now," Katie warned, looking highly annoyed again.

"I'm just trying to say I got upset because he was late for something so important to you. Nothing has changed."

Katie leaned forward, her elbows resting on the table and, gritting her teeth, said in an almost monotone, "Water under the bridge, Mom. That was years ago."

Her daughter was right, and Tessa was ashamed of allowing her own bitterness to spoil what should be a celebration. "For your sake, I'll try to leave it in the past." The deep hurts she'd tried to bury for the past eight years always tumbled to the surface whenever Mike was around, and Tessa already feared she wouldn't be able to keep her word.

Katie reached across Jim and gave her father's hand an affectionate squeeze. "You and Daddy may be separated and living apart, but he's still my dad and an important part of my life. You both are. You have to accept that, Mother."

"I know that, Katie." Long ago Tessa had begun imagining her daughter's wedding as a happy time—that she and Mike would be a good example for their daughter and her future husband to follow. She knew now just how miserably they had failed.

Acting as though he'd been ignoring their exchange, Mike picked up the menu and began to peruse it. "I'm sure your mother is as interested in hearing about this wedding as I am. When is it going to be? After your graduation?"

Katie giggled as her face brightened. "Oh, Daddy, I knew you'd be happy for us. No, not after graduation. It's going to be Christmas Day, and we—"

Her father closed the menu and stared at his daughter, open-mouthed. "*This* Christmas Day? That's only two weeks off." A smile tilted at his lips. "Oh, I get it! You're going to elope, and you want your mother and me to go with you, right? That sounds like fun. Where are we going?"

Again, she giggled. "No, silly, we're not going to elope! And yes, it's *this* Christmas!"

Finally, after sitting quietly during the bantering and arguing, Jim spoke up, his arm circling his beloved. "Katie wants to be married on Christmas Day, just like you two were."

"We were going to wait until I graduated in the spring." Katie leaned into Jim and smiled lovingly into his face before going on. "But we suddenly realized, if we'd hurry, we'd have time to plan the wedding and most of our close friends could attend since they'll be in town for the holidays. Isn't that a great idea?"

"But—"

Katie went on, "We already have our condo. And with us married it'll be much easier for me to concentrate on my studies this last semester instead of worrying about planning a wedding."

"But with going to school and your job and getting married, can you keep it all up?" Tessa asked, still not sure a Christmas wedding was a good idea.

Jim smiled confidently. "I want Katie to quit her job, Tessa.

Since I got my promotion at the construction company, I'm making enough now to support us both. This way she can spend all her time finishing up her schooling."

"And," Katie added, her excitement and enthusiasm bubbling over, "we've already talked to Pastor McIntosh and reserved the chapel at Seaside Community Church for Christmas Day. We'll have plenty of time to put up the decorations. The wedding is set for eight o'clock that evening."

"And," Jim said after giving his fiancée a quick peck on the cheek, "we have the chapel reserved for the rehearsal the evening of the twenty-third."

Katie grinned at her parents. "Pastor McIntosh said—"

Mike pursed his lips and shrugged. "Sounds to me like this wedding was going to happen whether your mother and I agreed to it or not. Looks like you two have things well in hand."

"But your wedding gown, Katie. . . What will you wear?" Tessa asked, still in shock over her daughter's announcement. She'd looked forward to her daughter's wedding day with eager anticipation for years, expecting they'd have months to plan and prepare for it. She'd wanted it to be the best wedding ever. Not the simple no-frills kind she and Mike had, but an all-out formal wedding.

Katie beamed. "Remember the gown I showed you in that bridal magazine when we were at your house for Thanksgiving? The one with the long train and the organza beaded bodice?"

Tessa nodded. She well remembered the dress. It was exactly the kind she would have picked for Katie. Expensive, yes, but this was her only daughter. That gown would be well worth the price.

"I called my friend Della at her bridal shop, and she said she could order it and it'd be here in three days! The very same dress! Isn't that just too cool?"

Tessa's jaw dropped. "Am I hearing you right? You're planning on having a *full formal* wedding? With all the trimmings? In only two weeks?"

Katie's smile broadened. "Uh-huh, just like the kind we've always talked about."

"With only two weeks to pull it together?" Tessa nearly choked, just saying the words.

"There's plenty of time," Katie said confidently. She paused long enough to take a deep breath then offered her mother a loving smile. "*If* you'll help me."

Still struggling for words, Tessa gave her head a slight nod. "You—you know I'll help you, dear, but—"

"Thanks. I knew I could count on you, Mom."

Mike unfolded his napkin and placed it on his lap. "Yeah, you can count on me, too, pumpkin. I'll help you in any way I can."

"You'll help? When would you ever find time?" Tessa asked, her voice laced with sarcasm she instantly regretted.

"Mother!"

"It's okay," Mike said, gesturing toward Tessa. "Old habits are hard for your mother to break."

"So, dear," Tessa said, forcing herself to ignore his comment and concentrate on the issue at hand, "who is going to be your maid of honor? And what about bridesmaids and a flower girl and a ring bearer? Invitations? There is so much to do. I'm not sure, even with my help, that you're going to be able to pull this off in fourteen days."

"We've already purchased our invitations. They should be ready by tomorrow." Katie reached into her purse, pulled out a list, and began to read. "Let's see. Valene Young will be my matron of honor, of course, since she's my best friend. I'm only having two bridesmaids—Valene's twin sister, Vanessa, since she's almost as close a friend as Val—and Della." She continued to check her list. "Do you think Carrie is old enough to be my flower girl?"

Tessa nodded. "That little cousin of yours is almost four now. I'm sure she'll be able to sprinkle rose petals with no trouble at all. Who else?"

"Ryan is nearly eight," Katie went on. "Do you think he'd act as ring bearer? I don't want to embarrass him."

Her father shrugged his broad shoulders. "Getting him to be the ring bearer might not be a problem, but getting him into a tux? I don't know about that."

Katie shot him a confident smile. "Well, you're his uncle. I'll bet you can convince him."

He returned her challenge with a consenting wink.

"Jim is asking Jordan Young, his best friend, to stand up with him. Nathan, Vanessa's husband, and Della's husband, Brandon, will be his groomsmen." She turned back to Mike. "You will give me away, won't you, Daddy?"

Mike blinked hard in a rare show of emotion. "Sure, honey. I'd be honored."

"Maybe not when you hear the rest of my request," Katie said as she glanced nervously from one parent to the other. "I want Mom to give me away, too."

"Is that proper?" Tessa asked, stunned by her daughter's strange request.

"Hey, it's their wedding. If she wants us both, I'm agreeable to it. What about you, Tessie?" Mike eyed his wife warily.

Tessa bit at her lip. Why did it always seem he was offering her a challenge? It was as if he enjoyed putting her on the spot every chance he got. Well, she'd show him! "I think it's a lovely idea. Of course, I'm agreeable. Now what other plans do you have?"

Katie seemed surprised her mother didn't offer any flack but didn't mention it and went on checking her list. "Mother, I know you're busy helping at Grandpa's plumbing shop so I'm going to take care of almost everything. The florist, the caterer, the photographer, the organist, and I'll ask Jane Moray to sing, of course. I love her voice. I'm going to ask her husband Keene, too, if he'll be in town. Wouldn't it be fabulous to have a famous opera singer like Keene sing at our wedding?" Katie paused thoughtfully. "I've already arranged for Valene and Vanessa to go to Della's bridal shop and choose their dresses." She turned to Jim. "You'll have to set up the tux fittings for the men, and don't forget one for Ryan."

Jim nodded. "Gotcha."

Then turning to her father, she added, "Daddy, you need to go, too, and—"

Mike stared at his still empty plate. "Whoa, I'm getting dizzy just thinking about all of this. Sounds to me like a lot still has to be done to pull off this wedding. Are you sure you two can handle it, honey? You'd better let me and your mother help with some of those things." He grinned. "Or wait until spring! You have enough to do just finishing up your last semester of college. You need to keep your nose to the grindstone if you want to be an architect and make the big bucks."

Tessa bit her lip, finding it almost impossible to not respond. *Oh, Mike. You offer to do something, then you disappear when it's time to do it. You've been that way as long as I can remember. I know you're going to disappoint her again.*

"Thanks, Daddy. If it weren't for you paying my tuition and other expenses, and the scholarships and grants I've qualified for, I wouldn't be able to be a full-time college student. Being an architect major is more work than I'd anticipated. But I'll make it. I have to, and someday I plan to pay you back." Katie tossed her father a confident smile as she patted his shoulder. "If I find I'm having trouble getting all of it done, I'll call and tell you. I just figured the holiday season was probably one of the busiest times of the year for you and—" She stopped abruptly when Mike's cell phone rang.

"You can forget about paying me back. I wouldn't take it anyway. Paying your way through college was the least I could do for my only daughter." He snatched the phone from his jacket pocket, extended the little antenna then put it to his ear. "Garrett here. Uh-huh. Uh-huh. Where? Call the coroner. I'm on my way."

Tessa shoved back from the table hard enough to make her chair squeak on the restaurant's highly polished hardwood floors. "Couldn't you have turned that thing off, Mike? This is an important time for your daughter! Surely the San Diego police force can get along without their star detective for at least one hour."

Obviously ignoring Tessa's remark, he rose from his chair and grabbed his coat. "Sorry, pumpkin, gotta go."

"I know. You don't have to explain, Daddy." Katie gave him an understanding smile.

"Sure, Mike, she's used to her father being gone at the important times of her life," Tessa snapped, silently chastising herself for breaking her word again as she forked up a small wedge of tomato from her untouched salad plate.

Katie slapped at her mother's arm. "Daddy can't help it if someone needs him. It's important, or they wouldn't have called him!"

Mike's unresponsive silence irked Tessa.

Smiling, Mike stretched out his hand to his prospective son-in-law. "Congratulations, Jim. You're getting the very best."

Still ignoring Tessa, which he seemed to be doing all too often for her satisfaction, he bent and gave his daughter an affectionate peck on the cheek.

"I'll help anyway I can, and don't worry about the cost. Let's do this wedding up right."

Then with an appeasing look Tessa couldn't understand—especially considering their earlier bickering—he told her with a sly grin and without raising his voice, "Nice to see you again, Tessie. You're lookin' good."

Caught off guard by his surprise compliment, which actually seemed sincere, Tessa stared at him, whispering only a timid, "Thank you."

"Too bad your dad had to leave early, honey," Jim said once Mike was gone, consoling Katie with a pat on her shoulder. "At least we got to tell him our good news."

Katie's fingers reached up and cupped his hand before turning to her mother, a deep frown furling at her brow. "Did you have to make that remark about him being gone at the important times?"

Tessa felt very small. She knew before she'd finished saying it that her comment had been snide and out of place. "For your sake, if for no other reason," she told Katie meekly, "I should've kept my mouth shut. I know that. But when I think about all the times—"

"Mother! Can't you drop that old subject? It's been hashed and rehashed hundreds of times. We're here to discuss my wedding, not beat up on Daddy."

ঠ

Mike arrived at his destination in less than five minutes. Although he'd tried to keep his mind on the information he'd been given over the phone, it kept wandering back to the restaurant.

Tessie. That woman could whip him into frenzy without even trying. They hadn't had a decent conversation in more than eight years.

He checked the rearview mirror and quickly pulled into a narrow alley, bringing his car to a stop near a battered blue Dumpster.

"Hated to call you," Hal Lester, the officer on duty explained as he hurried toward him, clipboard and pen in hand. "I heard you were having lunch with your daughter, but—"

"Don't worry about it." Mike shrugged. "It's part of my job. My daughter's used to it, but your call sure bothered her mother."

The man frowned as if confused. "I thought you've been divorced for years."

"Not divorced. Separated." Mike shoved his keys into his pocket with a sigh. "Might as well have been divorced, but she doesn't believe in it." He grimaced. "Actually, neither do I."

"It's tough. My wife has always hated me being a cop. I'm waiting for the day she gives me the old ultimatum. Her way or the highway, as they say. I'd sure hate to have to choose."

"Goes with the territory, my friend. Now," Mike added as he pulled out his notebook, "let's get at it." He put his hand on the man's shoulder, eager for a change of subject. "Who found our Jane Doe?"

The officer checked the notes on his clipboard. "Some teenage kid who was skipping school and milling around the neighborhood. Said he was looking in the Dumpster for aluminum cans. He was pretty shaken up." He gestured toward the black and white vehicle parked farther down the alley. "He's sitting in my car."

"Any ID on her?"

"Nope."

"Cuts or bruises?"

The man nodded as he pulled the woman's hair back from her face, exposing a mass of purple, green, and yellow bruises, some appearing to have been there for several days. "Oh, yeah. Big-time. Looks like she's been used as a punching bag."

"Just like the other Jane Does we've had in the past few months. We've got to catch this guy. The whole area is in a panic. I worry about my daughter crossing the campus at night. No woman is safe." Mike crouched down and stared at the woman. "I hate calls like this. Never get used to them, but someone has to do the job. Think what the world would be like if there weren't guys like us around who will. I look at this job as a calling. If I didn't, I'm not sure I could stay with it. Things like this make me sick to my stomach. Sometimes I wish I'd decided to be a plumber instead of a cop, like my wife wanted me to be."

Hal squatted down beside him. "I know. Me, too. I try to explain the importance of our job to my wife all the time, but all she can think about is the evenings I'm away from her and the kids, the weird hours we work, and the moods we're sometimes in because of what we've had to deal with during our shift. Not to mention the danger."

"I know exactly what you mean. Each time I left for work, Tessa was afraid I wouldn't come back. It became an obsession with her. It was all she could think about. Every siren she heard, she thought was an ambulance coming after me because I'd been shot. When the phone would ring, she expected to hear I had been killed in a gun battle. Her paranoia drove me crazy. I tried to explain to her I rarely even had to draw my gun, but she was too obsessed to listen. Eventually, her unfounded worries and my dedication to the job became the wedge that drove us apart and our marriage ended." With a sad shake of his head Mike stood, his gaze still pinned on the unknown woman who lay at his feet. "Enough of my sad tale. Guess we'd better get moving. Dealing with this Jane Doe situation ain't gonna get any easier."

&

Tessa sat at her desk at Calhoun's Plumbing, Heating, and Air-Conditioning, staring at the invoice in her hand, not really seeing it. Her mind was elsewhere. *A Christmas Day wedding?* she asked inwardly with a shake of her head. *That girl! I hope she realizes what she's getting herself into, planning a formal wedding in less than two weeks.*

"Good lunch with Katie?" Unannounced, Tessa's father strode into her office, dressed in his gray uniform with the Calhoun's Plumbing, Heating, and Air-Conditioning emblem sewn over the pocket. "How is that granddaughter of mine?"

Tessa turned to the man with a smile, still clutching the invoice in her hand. "She and Jim are getting married Christmas Day."

He perched himself on the corner of the desk and gave her a broad grin. "Eloping, huh? But when you elope aren't you supposed to keep it a secret from your parents?"

"They're not eloping, Dad. She's having a full formal wedding, complete with gown, bridesmaids, and men in tuxedos, at the church."

He took the invoice from her hand and placed it on a stack of papers, but she barely noticed. "You serious?"

"Ridiculously serious. She announced it at lunch."

"Guess that means you'll be taking some time off. Well, don't worry about it. The girls in the office can handle everything, and they can call you if they can't. I really appreciate you helping out like this while Caroline is on sick leave. It may be months before she's able to come back to work."

She nodded. "I hate to leave you high and dry, but thanks,

Dad. I have a feeling Katie will be needing all the help I can give her."

"Mike know yet?"

She propped her elbows on the desk and rested her chin in her palms. "He was there, too. She'd invited him."

He stood, walked around the desk, and slipped an arm about her shoulders. "I know that must have been difficult. But, Tessa, it's been eight years. You've got to get over your hard feelings toward Mike. That man has suffered, too, and he's going to be a part of your daughter's life as long as he's around."

She leaned into his side with a sigh. "I know. When Katie asked me to help her with her wedding and Mike volunteered to help, too, I behaved rather badly. Katie was pretty upset with me, and I don't blame her."

Her father took one of her hands in his and stroked it as he held it in his grasp. "Maybe it's time you divorced Mike and found someone else—"

"Someone else? Surely you don't mean that, Dad." She lifted her gaze to meet his. "I can't. The scriptures won't let me."

"Do you really think God expects you to spend the rest of your life alone?"

Tessa stared up into his eyes. Her father was a good man— one of the best. However, he had never felt the need to have God in his life. How well she remembered the last time she'd tried to share her faith with him. He'd made it perfectly clear he could get along just fine without God. He claimed he'd never done a single thing in his life he need be ashamed of, so he was convinced a God of love would never condemn him. He'd even asked Tessa to never bring up the subject again. She had resigned herself to trying to live the Christian life before him and let it be her witness. Why couldn't he understand the worst sin of all was to refuse God's love and sacrifice?

"You could always let Mike back into your life."

She pulled away from him. "Not after what he did!"

"Other than devoting his life to his job, exactly what did he do, Tessa, that would make you cast him aside like a old piece of jewelry you'd tired of? I know you worried about him all the time, but danger and the risk of injury go with his job. You knew that when you married him. Didn't you take vows at your wedding that said for better or for worse? Seems to me the *worse* part was Mike's job. I would think your God—"

"I'd rather not discuss it." How could she discuss it without admitting even though she had meant those vows at the time, she had been sure she could talk Mike into quitting the police force and take a simple nine-to-five job, one that wouldn't put him in danger?

He placed his hands on her shoulders and spun her around to face him. "Look, Katie's getting married. She's already moved out. You really don't want to spend the rest of your life rattling around in that big house all alone, do you?"

"I like that house." Though she hadn't given him a direct answer, she had given that very question more consideration than she cared to admit. Would she be happy living in that house alone? Especially since there was a chance that Jim might be transferred to another job out of town eventually? That house had been her home for more than twenty years. She'd never be comfortable living in an apartment or a condo. She loved that house. It was exactly what she and Mike had wanted—the house of their dreams.

Tessa drew in a deep breath and let it out slowly. The house on Forrest Street was no longer *his* home. It was stupid, she knew, but although the man had been out of her life for eight years now, she still thought of it as *their* home. Hers *and* Mike's. The nightstand on his side of the bed still contained every item it had held before he left, right down to the little dispenser of dental floss he used every night.

Why, she didn't know, but she could never get rid of those things. Even his suits and shirts still hung in the closets. He'd never asked for them, and she'd never been able to get rid of them. Occasionally, on long nights when Katie was sleeping soundly in her bed, Tessa would pull one of his suits from the rack and hold it close, savoring the faint lingering smell of his aftershave. Sometimes, she'd even wrap the sleeves about her shoulders and pretend he was holding her close.

"I know Gordon Banks has taken a liking to you," her father was saying. "Rod told me he invited you to have coffee with him after church Sunday evening. Maybe you ought to take him up on his offer. He's a good man, and he's been mighty lonely since he lost Sarah."

She yanked from his grasp and slowly made her way to the window, her eyes glazing over. "Even if I felt God would allow it, I could never love another man, Dad. Not the way I loved Mike."

Her father moved up behind her and gently began to knead her tense neck muscles then softly whispered into her ear. "Loved? Or still love?"

two

Don't be ridiculous!" Tessa shouted at her father, appalled by the idea. "Any love I had for Mike died long ago."

Mr. Calhoun raised a questioning brow. "Methinks the lady protests too much."

She gave him a flip of her hand. "Come on, Dad, don't you remember how Mike never had time for me or Katie? He was too busy playing detective. His job always came before his family."

He perched himself on the corner of her desk again and pulled a ballpoint pen from the mug where she kept them, eyeing it and twirling it between his fingers. "Did you say *playing*? I wouldn't exactly call putting your life in constant danger to protect the community *playing*. Seems like a ton of work to me. Dedicated work. Dangerous work."

"Exactly! Extremely dangerous work but he loves it, Dad—thrives on it. Even though he knew I was always crazy with worry, I doubt he ever considered the danger involved. His dad was a cop. He's a cop. He claims it's in his blood."

"As I recall, you knew that even before the first date you two had. I distinctly remember you telling me the first day you met him he'd told you he was going to be a cop, or did you forget that little fact?" After placing the pen back in its place, he sat quietly, as if expecting the outburst that was about to erupt.

"You're right, but that was before we started dating! If he loved me and knew how I felt about it, I was hoping he would change his plans."

"Oh? You actually thought his plans were going to change?

Just because he met you and you were squeamish about his chosen occupation?"

"My plans changed. I was going to be a nurse. I gave mine up for him!"

"Not the same thing."

She felt her anger rising. How dare he defend Mike! "Of course it's the same thing!"

"Nope. He couldn't have the babies."

"Have the babies? That gives him the right to take a job that allows him no time for his family and sets him up for possible death? Why was it my responsibility to be there twenty-four, seven? Where was he when Katie ran a fever, cut her teeth, or fell down and required stitches? Where was he when she was in the programs at school? Played team sports? Had teacher's conferences?" She rammed her finger into her chest. "I was the one who was there! The one who was both mother and father to her. The one who took her to church. Taught her right from wrong. Punished her when she needed it. Held her when she was afraid. Kissed her hurts away. Not Mike!"

He strode around the desk and slipped his arm about her shoulders. "Who made all those things possible?"

She pushed away and gazed up at him. "Who made all those things possible? What do you mean?"

"You were a stay-at-home mom, sweetie. Mike brought home the paycheck, paid the bills, and shielded you from the traumas of life. From what I've heard, he still is. Isn't he making the house payments and giving you a living allowance each month? And you're still covered by his insurance. I'm not sure you realize how lucky you have been. Many women would have given anything to stay at home like you did and be there for your child. Did you ever thank him for that?"

His words stunned her. "Thank him for letting me be a

mother to his daughter?"

"He was the one who went off to work every day."

Now her dander was up. "I worked, too! Probably as hard as he did. Raising a daughter is not an easy task. Especially without your husband being around to help."

"And being a cop isn't hard?"

There he was, her own father, taking Mike's side again. "He didn't *have* to be a cop. He could have come to work with you. I know you offered him a partnership in the plumbing shop. That was a very generous offer. He should have taken it."

Her father let out a chuckle. "Yes, I offered him a partnership, but only because you wanted me to. I knew he'd never accept it. Can you imagine Mike Garrett as a plumber? I sure can't!"

"If he truly loved me, he would have accepted your offer."

"If *you* truly loved him, knowing his lifelong dream was to be on the police force, perhaps you would have accepted him for who and what he was."

A lump rose in Tessa's throat, making it hard to speak without tearing up. "I truly loved Mike, Dad, and you're right. I did know—even before we were engaged—that Mike had already chosen his profession to ultimately become a San Diego detective. But I had foolishly hoped once we were married he would change his mind. But he never did. He never even considered it—not once—though I begged him over and over. Our life was one big argument. Can't you see? He was married to the force, never to me. When push came to shove, he chose being a detective over being my husband."

Mr. Calhoun pulled his daughter from her chair and wrapped his long arms about her, hugging her close. "Ask yourself this question, daughter. Who did the pushing and shoving? Who gave Mike the ultimatum that forced him to make a choice?"

Though she would never voice it, in her heart she answered, *Me*.

He lovingly stroked her hair as she rested her head on his shoulder. "Whoever did that pushing and shoving was the one who ended your marriage," he whispered into her ear. "Perhaps that same person could put it back together again—if she wanted to."

It's too late, her heart said. *Much too late. Our marriage has ended.* "Mike was more interested in the partners he's had over the years than he was in me!"

"Wasn't that remark a little childish?"

"I don't think so. It's true," she shot back defensively.

"Partners have a common bond, Tessa. It's important that they work closely together. Their lives may depend on that trust and bonding."

"He never talked to me about the things *I* cared about, but he seemed to know everything that was going on in his partner's life."

"Perhaps some of that was your fault," he told her in a kindly manner. "Maybe it was your fault as much as Mike's that the two of you never had time for each other."

Tessa's heartbeat quickened. "What do you mean by that remark?"

He held up his fingers and began to enumerate. "You were a soccer mom, president of the Parent-Teacher Association, leader of the weekly women's Bible study class, and helped with the church bulletin. You attended jazz exercise classes three days a week, lunched with your friends, took painting classes, chauffeured Katie to her ballet lessons, kept score for her T-ball games, baked cookies for dozens of projects, worked on the voter registration, helped Katie with their homework—all kinds of things. Who knows what else? No wonder the two of you rarely communicated. You barely saw one another. From my perspective—let's face it—you were as inaccessible as he was."

Tessa gave her head a violent shake. "That's not true! I would have put those things aside if Mike would have taken a regular job."

"Like being a plumber?"

"Yes! Like being a plumber!"

Mr. Calhoun let loose a slight snicker. "Guess you don't remember all the calls I got when you were young and our family sat down to dinner. From customers whose sinks had stopped up and they were having company and needed me to come and fix their problems right away to toddlers flushing toys down the toilet. Or the hot water tank was leaking. Or it was ninety degrees outside and their air conditioner conked out on them. I wish your mother were here. You could ask her. I don't know how many meals she had to warm over for me because some customer had a problem—many times on holidays. But you know what? She loved me, and she understood that my dad started Calhoun's Plumbing, Heating, and Air-Conditioning and it was my legacy. Did she ever tell you what I really wanted was to be a pilot?"

Tessa stared at him. "A pilot? You?"

"Yes, I had loved flying since I was a young boy and took my first flight, and I wanted more than anything to be a pilot. But that would have meant leaving home and joining the Air Force since that was the only way I could have afforded it. I'll never forget the day I told my dad I didn't want to be a plumber. It nearly broke his heart. It was only after I found out how much he had sacrificed to start the company he had wanted to pass on to his son—me—that I knew I could never do anything but follow in his footsteps. Though my desire to be a pilot never left me, I can honestly say I have never regretted giving it up. The love and sacrifice my father made for me was far more important than any old dream. That man worked round the clock, seven days a week, to get this company going. Like you resented the time Mike gave to his job, I resented the time my father gave to his. I remember one time, especially, when he didn't show up at the most important football game of my life. I was so mad when I saw my mom sitting in the stands by herself I threw my helmet at the wall hard enough to crack it."

"Why wasn't he there?" Tessa asked, amazed at the emotion displayed on her normally emotionless father's face.

"His biggest client's toilet stopped up while he was entertaining some important people. He called my dad and demanded he come right then, or he was going to pull all his business from him. Dad had promised to buy me a new car for graduation and knew if he lost that account, he wouldn't be able to do it. So, not wanting to disappoint me, he fixed the stool and missed my game. Later, he told me it was the hardest decision of his life. Whatever he chose, one way or the other, I would be disappointed. I felt like a heel when I found out about it."

Tessa weighed his words thoughtfully. "That's so sad. The poor man."

"Mike didn't leave you or Katie to go play golf or take up a hobby. He left you for his job. A job he loved, despite the danger and long hours involved. I doubt you or I, or anyone who isn't a cop, have any idea of the dreadful things he faces every day. He meets the slime of the earth on their turf, not knowing when one of them is going to turn on him and perhaps put his life in jeopardy. Think what the world would be like without people like Mike. Not many are willing to put their own life on the line to protect the rest of us. Because of Mike and others like him, we live relatively safe lives, leaving them to deal with those who would cause us harm."

"You make him sound like a saint."

Ben Calhoun slowly made his way to the door, pausing and turning toward her as he reached for the knob. "I don't know much about saints, but I know a good man when I see one. Mike Garrett was, and is, a good man. The years are slipping away from both of you, Tessa. If you have any feelings left for Mike, I'd suggest you try to reconcile with him."

"Reconcile with Mike? How can you even say that?"

He sent her a tender smile. "Like I asked you before, don't you think that God of yours would expect you to work things out with your husband? Besides, nothing would make your daughter any happier than to see her parents together. Think about it."

Before she could give him all the other reasons reconciliation would not be possible, nor was she interested in one, he stepped through the door, closing it securely behind him.

Tessa stared at the closed door, startling when the phone rang. "Calhoun's Plumbing, Heating, and Air-Conditioning. Tessa Garrett speaking. How may I help you?"

"I think we need to talk. How about having dinner with—"

"Mike? Is that you?"

"Yeah, it's me." The voice on the other end was unmistakable.

"I—I don't think that would be wise." Why was her stomach doing flip-flops?

"Even if I promise to behave myself and act like a gentleman?"

"What do we have to talk about that we haven't already said?"

"Come on, Tessie. Our daughter is getting married. Can't we put our differences aside for the next two weeks and be civil to one another? Is that asking too much, knowing how pleased Katie would be to see us getting along for a change?"

"Are you sure you could work it into your busy schedule?" The old sarcasm tinged her words and tasted bitter to her lips.

"What I meant was," she said softly, "I wouldn't want to keep you from—"

"You name the time, and I'll be sure to be there."

There were a few things about the wedding they needed to discuss. Perhaps doing it face-to-face would be better than trying to do it over the phone. "About six thirty?"

"Six thirty is fine."

"Where shall I meet you?"

"I could pick you up," he offered.

"I—I guess that would work, if you're sure it won't inconvenience you," she said, taking care to say it politely.

"No inconvenience at all. I'll see you at six thirty. Maybe we can have dinner at that Mexican restaurant in the mall."

She couldn't help smiling. That restaurant was one of her favorites. "That'd be nice. I'll be ready."

Tessa changed her clothes four times before she decided on a simple navy blue pantsuit and silver jewelry then settled into the chair in the living room, her hands locked together in her lap, as nervous as she'd been waiting for Mike before their first date.

Six thirty arrived, and no Mike.

Six forty-five, and still no Mike.

I knew it! I knew he wouldn't make it. This is just another one of his hundreds of broken promises.

When the clock on the mantel chimed seven, she rose, kicked off her shoes, and headed to the kitchen to make a sandwich, glad that Katie wasn't there to see how angry she was.

At seven thirty, the phone rang.

"Sorry, Tessie. I was within two blocks of our house when a call came in about an armed robbery in progress at that convenience store down on the corner. I was the closest one so I answered the call. I was sure glad I did. I was actually able to apprehend the guy when he came running out. He'd shot the young clerk behind the counter. I told the kid I'd go get his mother and bring her to the hospital. The poor woman took the news pretty hard so I stayed with her until another family member could get to the hospital and take over."

Tessa squeezed her eyelids tightly together and clamped her lips. He'd done it again. Put total strangers' needs first.

"I know I should have called you, but the boy's mother was crying so hard, all I could think about was trying to comfort her," he went on without missing a beat. "The doctor said he's going to make it, but it was touch and go for a while. We can still make a late dinner."

She released a heavy sigh. "Forget it, Mike. I've made myself a sandwich."

"I'm sorry, Tessie. Really I am. I had no idea something like this was going to happen."

"You never did, Mike, but duty calls, and you always answer, no matter what."

"How about tomorrow night?"

She gave her head a sad shake. "No, not any night. Nothing's changed. Tomorrow night it'd just be somebody else who needs you while I sit and wait."

"Come on, Tessie. Give me a break. You didn't expect me to ignore the call for help, did you? Or to leave that wounded boy? Or not volunteer to get his mother and take her to the hospital?"

"Mike, I expect nothing out of you. I can't. I refuse to allow myself to be hurt again."

"But we need to talk."

"Let me put it this way: I'm going to do everything I can to help Katie with her wedding. When, and if, you have a few minutes to spare, you are welcome to assist me. Otherwise, I'll go on without you. I will not let you ruin our daughter's wedding because of some detail you may not have had time to take care of."

"I'll be there, Tessie. I promise. I want to do what I can to make her wedding the kind of wedding she deserves."

"You shouldn't make promises you can't keep, Detective Mike Garrett. I should think you'd know that by now. Now, if you don't mind, I'd like to finish my sandwich."

"Sure. Yeah, go ahead. I'll catch you later. You know you can call me anytime, don't you?"

"Good night, Mike."

"Night, Tessie."

Slowly, Tessa placed the phone back in its cradle, glanced at the half sandwich on the plate, and then picked it up and tossed it into the trash. *Reconciliation, Dad? No way!*

❧

Mike closed the lid on his flip phone, cutting the connection.

"Hey, Mike. You still here? I thought you were having dinner with your ex-wife tonight."

He turned toward one of the EMTs who'd brought the boy into the hospital making his way toward him. "Yeah, I was, but it didn't work out."

The man put a hand on his shoulder. "Too bad. I kinda got the idea you were really looking forward to it."

Mike nodded. "I was."

"Wanna go home with me? My wife's got a platter of fried chicken waiting."

Mike gave him a smile then grew serious. "Thanks for the invitation, but no. You go on home, but let me give you a piece of advice. Don't let your job consume your life like I've done. Women don't understand our dedication. They need us there. Be there for your woman or, take it from me, she won't be there for you. I always thought I was doing the right thing—even defended it. Now I'm not so sure."

The man stuck out his hand. "Thanks for the advice, Mike. Me and my wife have been having conversations about the same thing lately. I love her, and I sure don't want to lose her. No job, no matter how important it is, is worth that."

Mike took the man's hand and gave it a vigorous shake. "Remember that and you'll get along fine. Life stinks without the people you love in it. It's taken me all these years to find that out. It's too late for me, but you're still young. Don't blow it like I did."

He watched as the handsome EMT headed for the ambulance. *Take my advice, kid. Cherish what you've got while you still have it with you, 'cause once you lose it you may never get it back.*

ð

Tessa turned out the kitchen light and made her way toward the stairs, deciding to go to bed early, too angry to even try to read the book on her nightstand, the one she'd picked up at the bookstore earlier that week and had been eager to read. When she reached the top of the landing, the phone rang again. Thinking it was Mike she raced back down the stairs to answer it, snatched it up, and shouted an impatient, "Hello."

"Tessa?"

She recognized the voice immediately.

"This is Jim. I have bad news. Katie and I are at the hospital. She tripped over a skateboard one of the neighbor kids left in the parking lot and broke her ankle."

"Oh, Jim, that's awful! Is she in much pain?"

"Yeah, quite a bit. I was sure glad I was with her. I carried her to the car. She wants you to come. We're in the emergency room at Community Hospital."

"I'll be right there, Jim. Thanks for calling."

"Could you call Mike and tell him? In my haste, I left my

cell phone behind and had to use the pay phone in the hall. I really want to get back to Katie."

Call Mike? After the conversation we had tonight? He did say to call him anytime. "Sure, I'll call him. You get back to Katie and tell her I'll be there right away."

Tessa ended their conversation then fed in Mike's cell phone number. "Jim just phoned and asked me to call you. Katie fell and broke her ankle. She's in the emergency room at Community Hospital. I'm heading there now."

"I'm on my way, too. Poor kid. I wonder what this will do to their wedding plans."

"I have to go. I need to get to Katie." Without even adding a good-bye, she hung up the phone then grabbed her car keys and purse from the table and rushed toward the door.

Katie was lying on a gurney in a crowded cubicle when Tessa entered, her cheeks stained with tears, dark rings under her eyes where her mascara had run from all the crying. "I'm sorry to be such a baby, Mom, but it hurt. I can't believe something so stupid as tripping on a skateboard could happen to me. I'd like to wring that kid's neck."

Tessa cradled her daughter's hand in hers, stroking her knuckles lovingly with her thumb. "I know, honey. I'm so sorry this happened. Was it a bad break?"

"They've taken X-rays. The doctor should be back soon with more information," Jim volunteered from the other side of the bed, his face contorted with concern.

"How's my girl?" Mike rushed into the tiny cubicle and bent to kiss his daughter's forehead.

A fresh tear ran down Katie's cheek. "I'm okay now, Daddy. This whole thing is a nightmare."

"She tripped over a skateboard someone had left in the parking lot," Tessa explained, suddenly remembering she hadn't taken time to fill him in on how it had happened.

"The name and address of the kid who left it there were written on the bottom of the skateboard," Jim said, crowding in and patting Katie's hand. "I'm going to have a talk with his parents."

"Want me to do it?" Mike asked, leaning to kiss Katie's forehead again. "I'll put a little fear into the kid. He won't leave that thing lying around again, I assure you."

"Sure, sir, if you want to."

"Show him your badge; that'll scare him," Tessa blurted out without thinking.

Mike turned and gave her a hard look. "You're great at those zingers, aren't you?"

Katie let out a moan. "Please, you two! Can't you stop? I'm hurting. I don't need this!"

"I'm sorry, baby." Tessa wished she could take back her remark. "It slipped out. I shouldn't have said it."

"I'm sorry, too, pumpkin. I had no business responding like that. I should have kept my mouth shut and not let her get to me."

"Well, I see your family has arrived." A middle-aged balding man in a white lab coat moved in between Mike and Jim. "I have some good news and some bad news. The good news is it's a clean break and should heal nicely with time. The bad news is you will need to stay off that leg until the swelling goes down and we can put a cast on it. Then, if all goes well, you'll be on a walking cast in a week or so. Maybe less. I hope you didn't have any plans to go skiing over the holidays."

"We're getting married on Christmas Day," Katie explained tearfully, wiping her cheeks with the back of her hand.

The doctor grimaced. "Oh? What bad timing for an accident. You'll probably want to put that wedding on hold for a while."

"No, I don't want to put it on hold," Katie said firmly, shaking her head. "I want to get married on Christmas Day, just like my parents did, and I'm not going to wait a full year."

"But, honey," Tessa began, "you can't get married wearing a cast."

"Why not?" Mike asked. "She's going to wear a long dress. No one is going to see it anyway."

"It's not the cast," Tessa shot back, wondering whatever possessed him to make such an outlandish statement. "Preparing for the kind of wedding Katie wants takes time and lots of planning, not to mention all the running around, making selections, and picking things up. She'll be confined to bed for several days and then have a cast on her ankle. There's no way she can do all those things!"

"Why not? She's got us! The two of us can do what she needs to do."

Filled with frustration, Tessa glared at him. "Us? You and me? You mean *me*, don't you? She'd never be able to count on you!"

"Mom!"

"I mean it, Katie. He was supposed to take me to dinner tonight to discuss your wedding. He promised he'd be there. Did he make it? No! More than an hour after he had arranged to be there, he phoned to say—once again—his job had kept him from making it."

"I couldn't help it. I was the closest one to an in-progress armed robbery. I had to take the call," Mike explained in his defense as he leaned over the bed.

"You aren't the only member of the San Diego Police Department, Mike. Someone else could have taken that call. Be honest. You wanted to take it. You're like an old fire horse that gets all excited when the fire alarm goes off. It's in your blood. Admit it!"

The doctor looked from one to the other, frowning, then

cleared his throat. "We need to get Katie's ankle immobilized now. You folks can continue your discussion in the waiting room or outside."

Tessa started to protest but realized the doctor was right. All she and Mike were doing was upsetting their daughter. "I'm sorry. Let me know if Katie wants me," she told Jim as she kissed her daughter then exited the cubicle.

"I'll be in the waiting room, too," Mike said in an almost whisper. "Forgive me, Katie."

He followed Tessa to a room filled with chairs. The only two seats available were side by side in a far corner. They seated themselves but remained silent.

"Aren't you Katie's parents?" a young woman holding a baby asked.

Tessa nodded.

"I saw Jim bring her in. Too bad about her ankle. I hope this doesn't interfere with their wedding plans. She told me all about it when I saw her at the grocery store this afternoon. I live in the same group of condos."

"We're not sure about the wedding yet," Tessa answered, glad Katie had such a concerned neighbor.

"She's lucky to have the two of you. My parents are divorced. They can't be in the same room without starting a big argument and hurling angry words at each other."

Tessa glanced at Mike and found him staring at her. "We both love her very much."

"Well, here comes my friend. She burned her hand on the stove so I brought her in. Looks like she's ready to go home. It's been nice meeting you. Give Katie my love."

"We will. Nice to meet you, too." Tessa gave a little wave as the girl, her baby, and her friend departed.

"Why didn't you tell her *we* can't be in the same room

either?" Mike asked, picking up a sports magazine from a side table.

"Because I'm embarrassed to admit it. It's your fault, you know. I thought we'd agreed to a truce."

"You sure didn't keep your part of the bargain. You tore into me like a wet hen when I phoned to tell you why I didn't show up tonight."

She huffed and turned her head away. "I had every right to tear into you. As usual, you broke your promise. I don't know why I ever expected you to show up. Not with your track record."

Mike idly flipped through the pages of the magazine, finally closing it and placing it back on the table. "I deserved that comment, but not because I intentionally broke my promise. Only because I didn't call sooner to let you know why I would be late. I fully intended to take you to dinner tonight." He pointed to his shirt. "I put on this stupid blue polo shirt because you used to tell me you liked me in blue." He offered a bashful grin. "I even bought you a bouquet of flowers. They're still out in my car."

Her eyes widened with surprise. "You bought me flowers?"

He nodded. "Yes. Red roses. Your favorite."

"That's because the first corsage you ever gave me was made of red roses and white carnations."

"You remember that?"

She tried to control the tiny smile that threatened to erupt but failed. "Of course, I remember. You were so cute, standing in my parents' doorway, holding that corsage. You even pinned it on my dress."

He laughed. "I stuck you with the pin."

She laughed, too. "Yes, you did. I tried not to flinch, but I couldn't help it. I was afraid I'd bleed on my white dress."

"I felt all thumbs."

"I was nervous, too."

"You were so beautiful. You—you still are."

"And you were very handsome. I'd never seen you in a suit before."

"I spent every penny I made working at the grocery store that week to buy that suit and your flowers. I was so afraid you'd want to go out for a hamburger and fries after the party. All I had left were two one-dollar bills."

"We had such a good time that night, didn't we?"

He nodded. "The best. You were the prettiest girl there. I couldn't believe you were my date. All the guys envied me."

"All the girls envied me. You were dashingly handsome."

"What happened to us, Tessie? Where did we go wrong?"

His question kindled the old fire of resentment. "How dare you ask me that? You cut me out of your life, Mike. You cut our family out of your life. It was no longer you and me against the world. Everything was what *you* wanted. My wants and desires went by the wayside."

"What I wanted? Everything I did, I did for us, Tessie!"

"Oh? I wanted you to become a cop? Work weird hours. Be gone from me all hours of the day and night? Put your life in jeopardy?"

"Those weird hours on those weird shifts no one else wanted to work were what made it possible for you to stay home with Katie. I thought *that* was what you wanted!"

She bristled. "What I wanted—was you! I missed you, Mike. I—I loved you!"

"You loved me? If you loved me so much, why did you make my life miserable?"

"I made *your* life miserable? What did you have to be miserable about? You were working your dream job, having fun with your cohorts, flaunting your badge around the bad boys while I stayed home with a sick baby cutting teeth and crying into all hours of the day and night."

"Every cent I ever made went into our joint account. Did I ever complain about the way you spent my money?"

"Excuse me." They both looked toward a young woman who was sitting nearby, cradling her fussing baby. "My son is not feeling well, and I'm trying to get him back to sleep."

Tessa nodded and wished she could crawl into a hole. "I'm sorry. Our daughter broke her ankle tonight. I—I guess we're both a little unnerved."

"Yes, I'm sorry, too," Mike said.

The woman gave them a smile then turned her attention back to her son.

"Sorry, Tessie. When will I learn to keep my big mouth shut?"

She blinked back tears of regret. "My fault, too."

They sat silently, each pretending to read a magazine that held nothing of interest to either of them. Tessa had to smile when she realized the magazine in her hand was about wrestling and Mike's magazine was one about foods.

Finally, Jim appeared. "They're going to release her as soon as they have her prescription for pain meds and paperwork ready. Why don't you two go on home? There's nothing more you can do here."

Mike stood, his long arms dangling awkwardly by his sides. "Won't you need help getting her back to the condo?"

"No. Val and Jordan will be there by the time I get her home. Valene insists on staying with her tonight, and Vanessa will tomorrow night, if she needs someone there. We'll take good care of her."

"I could stay with her," Tessa volunteered. "They have husbands to care for."

Jim placed his hand on her arm. "It's already settled. She'll be fine. I'll have her call you in the morning."

Tessa felt Mike's arm slip about her shoulders—a familiar sensation she'd sorely missed but would never dare admit aloud.

"She'll be fine, Tessie. Don't worry. Jim and her friends will take good care of her."

She smiled up into Mike's reassuring face. "I know they will. That's very nice of them to help."

He took her hand in his and tugged her to her feet. "I'll walk you to your car."

"I'd like that." Her hand still tucked into her husband's, she gave Jim a smile and a wave. "Call if she needs me."

Though no words were exchanged as they crossed the parking lot, Tessa felt a warmth and safety she hadn't felt in a long time as Mike continued to hold her hand. When they reached her car he took her keys and opened her door. Tessa crawled in then tossed her purse onto the passenger seat, feeling as awkward as a bowlegged ballerina. "Thanks, Mike."

He closed the door then rested his hands on the ledge when she rolled down the window, stooping to meet her gaze. "My pleasure."

"Do you really think she'll be all right?"

"I'm sure of it."

Tessa dipped her head shyly. "Remember when I broke my arm? You had to change Katie's diapers."

He chuckled. "I remember. Poor kid couldn't keep them on. I could never get those tapes stuck on right."

"You tried. That's all that mattered."

"That was before I made detective. After that, I barely made it home long enough to take a shower and catch a little shut-eye."

She nodded. "I had so hoped making detective would give you regular hours. Guess I was pretty naïve."

"Don't forget, making detective meant a big increase in pay. I doubt you would have been able to stay home with the Katie and maintain our lifestyle without that extra pay."

"But it took you away from us."

"After a little while, it seemed you didn't care. Your life was full without me."

"I filled it with those things only because you didn't have time for me!"

Mike stood and rested his flattened palms on the roof of her car. "Our life sounds like a dog chasing its tail. The faster he chases it, the further it seems out of his reach, and he runs even faster. Our lives were like that, weren't they? You weren't there because I worked long hours, and I worked long hours because you didn't seem to care."

Tessa leaned her head toward the window, her gaze locking with his. "Do you have any idea how frightened I was? Knowing you were out there on the streets? Being the possible target of some criminal's bullet? Putting your life on the line when other fathers were home with their wives and children? No wonder the divorce statistics are so high among law enforcement officers. I often thought divorce might be the best thing for us. I couldn't live like that, Mike. Never knowing where you were or what was happening to you."

"I didn't think you believed in divorce."

"I don't, but perhaps it would have made things easier—for both of us."

He cupped his hand around her wrist and leaned toward her. "Tessie, I haven't been to church in years, but I want you to know I still believe in God. You and I may not be together, but that doesn't mean I'd have the right in God's sight to marry another woman. Nor have I ever wanted to. You're the only woman I've ever loved."

"I find that hard to believe. If you loved me as you say you did, why wouldn't you accept my father's offer? He's made a good living, and you know he wanted to pass his business on down to the two of us."

"Me—a plumber?"

"Being a plumber wouldn't have been so bad. It's an honorable profession."

Mike paused, staring at her with a look she almost considered disgust. "You've never forgiven me for saying no to your father and staying with the San Diego PD, have you?"

"I—I guess not. Rejecting that job was like you were rejecting me."

"Tessie, turning down your father's unselfish offer was never meant to be a rejection of you, but in all sincerity, I never could understand why you couldn't see my side of things. It hurt me that you wanted me to become something I never wanted to be, and give up the job I've dreamed of having ever since I was a kid."

She covered her face with her trembling hands, her heart pounding in her ears. "I'm sorry, Mike. I know you've always wanted to be a cop, but I never wanted to be a cop's wife!"

He backed away, stuffing his hands in his pockets and shaking his head sadly. "Then I guess we're still at a standstill. We've never seen eye-to-eye on this, and I guess we never will."

She nodded. "No, I guess we won't."

"Good night, Tessie."

"Good night, Mike."

three

Despite the late hour, the phone was ringing when Tessa entered the house. It was her closest and dearest friend and fellow Christian, Ellen Zobel. The two women had been friends since high school, and now their daughters were close friends.

"I started trying to call you as soon as I heard about poor Katie's accident. How awful! Was the break very bad? Will she need to have surgery?"

Though weary and still trembling from her encounter with Mike, Tessa smiled faintly into the phone. She could always count on Ellen to be there when she needed her. How wonderful it was to have a friend like her. "Actually, it was a clean break and should heal fine. They're going to send her home, and Val's going to stay with her tonight."

"Yeah, Jim called Valene and Jordan from the hospital. He told them you and Mike were there."

Snapping the switch on the lamp on the end table, filling the room with light, Tessa sat down in the recliner that had been Mike's. "Things were a bit tense between Mike and me at first," she told her friend in a shaky voice, "but after a few words neither of us should have said, we settled down and actually had a fairly civil conversation."

"I'm glad to hear that. I know you hate for me to say it, sweetie, but both Bill and I think you and Mike were made for each other."

Tessa closed her eyes and took a deep breath before answering. "You wouldn't have thought so if you'd heard the ugly words we said to each other after we left the hospital. I can't help it, Ellen, I still hurt. Even now, eight years later."

"I know, honey. Being that close to Mike again, especially in a tense situation like Katie's accident, must have been difficult for both of you," Ellen said with genuine concern in her voice. "Jim said you had agreed to help with the wedding, but I guess now that Katie has broken her ankle they'll put it off for a while."

"Not unless they've changed their minds since Mike and I left the hospital. That stubborn daughter of ours has her heart set on a Christmas Day wedding, and she refuses to budge, despite her accident."

"What's Jim think about that?"

Tessa huffed. "You know Jim. Whatever Katie wants is fine with him. I don't know how we're ever going to pull things together that quickly, but we're going to try. Dad says he can spare me at the office, so I'll be free to do whatever she can't do herself."

"Well, it looks like you've got a big job ahead of you. Let me know if there is anything I can do to help. Valene and I have been looking through bridal magazines for ideas for the bridesmaids' dresses. I guess you know Val is going to be Katie's matron of honor and Vanessa and Della will be her bridesmaids."

"Yes, she told me, and she also said Jim had asked Jordan to be best man and Nathan and Della's husband to be his groomsmen. I'm so pleased our children are such close friends." Tessa let loose a nervous giggle. "Oh, by the way, I'm not the only one who has offered to help. Her father volunteered his services, too."

"Mike?"

"Yep, Mike. The man who thinks the San Diego Police Department can't function without him. I don't know how he's going to find the time with the crazy hours he works. When he's on a case he doesn't stop until it's solved. He'll probably end up fizzling out on her like he has all her life but, knowing how that girl dotes on her father, she'll probably forgive him like she always has, and I'll end up doing everything without him."

"Well, like I said, I'm willing to do anything I can to help, and I'm sure Valene and Vanessa will, too, and you know I'll be praying for you, Katie, *and* Mike."

Tessa released a long pent-up sigh. "Thanks for calling, Ellen. I covet your prayers. These next two weeks are going to be trying, to say the least."

"You'll make it. You're the perfect organizer. With God on your side, how can you fail? Just don't let being around Mike get to you. Love you, sweetie. Get some rest. See you at church Sunday."

Tessa turned off the lamp then sat in the chair in the dark, thinking over the events of the day. Amazing! And with only two weeks to plan a wedding, the bride had broken her ankle. To top it all off, Mike had offered to help with the wedding plans. She lifted misty eyes heavenward, remembering the hurts of so long ago, hurts she had never been able to forgive. *God, please! I'll never get through this without Your help.*

⋙

Mike pulled a wad of keys from his pocket and after inserting the proper one into the keyhole gave it a twist and pushed the door open. It'd been a long day, and he was tired. He tossed his jacket onto a chair then made his way through his cluttered apartment into the tiny kitchen. Searching the cabinet for a clean cup and finding none, with a shake of his head, he pulled a dirty one from the sink and rinsed it beneath the faucet before filling it to the brim with water.

"Gotta clean this place up sometime," he told Felix, the

stray cat someone had placed in his car as a joke while he was interrogating a burglary suspect.

Felix sat in the middle of the kitchen floor, preening himself and ignoring his owner's comment.

"Don't care how dirty it gets, huh? Just so long as I make sure you have food and water, with an occasional cleaning of your litter box."

Still Felix ignored him.

"Want a cup of coffee? I hate drinking alone."

Without even a glance in his direction, Felix turned away and walked regally out of the room, his tail arched high over his back.

"I guess that means you don't want coffee." Mike placed the cup in the microwave then punched a few buttons. Once the water was hot, he pulled the jar of coffee granules from the cabinet, scooped in several spoonfuls, and gave it a stir. "Umm, that smells good. Nothing like a good strong cup of coffee at the end of a lousy day."

He grabbed a bag of stale doughnuts from the counter and carried them, along with the coffee, into the living room. After shoving a pile of old newspapers off the end table and onto the floor, he placed both the bag and the cup on its marred surface. "Tessie would have a fit if she could see this table. She always made sure I had a coaster under my cup."

He pulled a doughnut from the sack, broke it in half, and dunked the larger portion into his coffee before stuffing it into his mouth. "Stale doughnuts and instant coffee—what a meal. I wonder what Tessie is having for supper. Probably leftover roast beef, or maybe a thick slice of ham between two slices of the famous garlic-onion bread she makes in that bread maker of hers. Maybe even a wedge of lemon meringue pie for dessert."

His mouth watered just thinking about it. The last time he'd had a piece of Tessie's homemade lemon meringue pie was eight years ago, just a few days before she had ordered him to move out. She'd baked one for his birthday—a tradition, since he'd rather have lemon meringue pie any day than a standard birthday cake. Now that he lived alone, each year on his birthday, he had to settle for either a store-bought pie or pick one up at the little diner a few blocks from his apartment, neither of which could even begin to compare with Tessie's pie.

Felix jumped up onto the sofa, curled up on one of its loose cushions, and lay staring at him.

"She was a good wife, Felix—the best. She made our home a haven. Took great care of our daughter, too. I loved that woman, but I guess I never told her. I just supposed she knew."

He dunked the other half. "She never understood me, you know. Always complaining about the time I was away from home. Griped about the times I missed supper—the weird hours I worked. I thought she'd be happy when I made detective, but she wasn't. I have to admit the hours I work as a detective are even worse than when I worked the streets, but detective work is different. The bad guys don't keep office hours. You gotta get them when you can. She never understood how I could pull an all-night surveillance, then go back to work the next day, sometimes without even taking time to come home for a shower."

Felix stretched out on the pillow and closed his eyes.

"That's okay. Don't listen. I'm used to being ignored." Mike took the final swig of coffee then twisted the top on the doughnut sack. "Did she care that I had a dozen commendations on my office wall? Did she care that the mayor awarded me a medal of honor for bravery? That I made sure I crossed every

T and dotted every *I* when I worked a case, so the lawyers couldn't dispute the evidence?"

He shrugged his shoulders. "What am I saying? Of course she cared. She was the one who made sure those commendations were framed and hung on the wall. I guess she had a right to complain—sometimes. I did miss most of my kid's ball games, and I don't remember making one teacher conference with her. The thing that seemed to aggravate her the most was when I quit going to church with her. But my work was important. Why couldn't she see that?"

He pushed down the lever on the dilapidated recliner and allowed the footrest to lift his feet. "Tessie sure looked good today. How long has it been since I've seen her smile?" He pulled off his glasses and rubbed his eyelids.

Twisting to one side, he tugged his billfold from his hip pocket, pulled out a small snapshot, and stared at the image. "You were only about twenty-five when this picture was taken, Tessie—a real knockout. I was a fool to let you go."

Mike cradled the photograph to his chest and closed his eyes. Within minutes, he was asleep.

⁂

Tessa could stand it no longer. At eight thirty the next morning, she phoned Katie's apartment, determined to make sure her daughter was okay.

"Good morning, Valene. How's Katie today? Is she awake yet?"

"Morning, Tessa. She's doing great. I'm taking the phone to her so she can tell you herself. Here she is," Valene told her.

"I'm fine, Mom. My ankle barely hurts. The pain meds are really helping. Valene is taking good care of me," Katie told her. "Can you come over right away? I've already made a list of the things you can do for me. Like picking up the invitations, checking with the florist, and stopping by the caterer, and selecting the punch bowl for the reception. Val already has her hands full with just trying to help me get from room to room!" she added with a chuckle.

"I'd love to help out. Give me an hour to run a load of laundry through the washer and do up a few things around the house, then I'm yours for the rest of the day. Okay?"

"Thanks, Mom. You're the best. By the way, how did you and Daddy get along last night? Jim said he saw Dad walking you out to your car. I hope you two didn't get into another argument."

Remembering the more pleasant parts of their conversation, Tessa smiled. "We did all right."

"Well, come over as soon as you can. Della's shop is supposed to deliver my wedding gown sometime this morning. I can hardly wait. Can you believe in just two weeks I'll be a married woman?"

"Sure you don't want to postpone your wedding?"

Katie giggled into the phone. "Not a chance. This wedding is going to go off on schedule if I have to go down the aisle in a wheelchair."

"That's my impulsive Katie! See you in an hour or so. Love you."

"Love you, too, Mom. Bye."

Tessa loaded the washer, cleaned the kitchen, ran the sweeper in the family room, and then dressed for the day in a pair of jeans and her favorite T-shirt. After tossing the clothes into the dryer and pressing the button, she grabbed her keys and was heading for the door when the phone rang.

"Mom! Help!"

Tessa tightened her grip on the phone. "Katie? What's wrong? Are you okay? Is it your ankle?"

four

My ankle is fine. It's my dress!"

Tessa listened helplessly as Katie began to sob on the other end. "Your dress? What are you talking about?"

"My beautiful wedding gown! It arrived a few minutes ago. It's the wrong size!"

Tessa breathed a sigh of relief. "Oh, honey, don't worry. Maybe we can alter it."

"It's three sizes too small!" Katie blurted out between sobs. "Someone put the wrong tag on it! What'll I do? I phoned Della, and she said her supplier's orders are backlogged so she can't get another one. It was just a fluke that this one was available. I've called at least another six shops and no one else has it! I had my heart set on that dress."

Tessa racked her brain for a solution. "Maybe we could find a similar one."

"I can't go shopping! The doctor said I have to keep my leg elevated until the swelling goes down and I can get a walking cast on it!"

"Do you still have that picture of the dress? The one in the magazine?"

Katie sniffled loudly. "Yes."

"Maybe I could take it to Della's shop and try to find one something like it, in the right size."

"Would you?"

"Of course, I will. I'll come and get that picture and start my search. I'll bet I can find one you'll like every bit as much.

Maybe Della will let me bring several of them home for you to see."

Tessa picked up the list and photograph at Katie's then hurried to Della's shop.

"Mrs. Garrett, how nice to see you again," Della said.

"Della, we've been on a first-name basis for years."

"I know, but I prefer being more formal in my shop, even with close friends. It sets a more professional, respectful tone toward all of our customers. Anyway, Katie called and said you were on your way. I can't tell you how sorry I am about the mix-up. Someone at the factory must have put the wrong size tag on the dress when it was constructed. I called them, hoping to get a replacement, but they didn't have another one in stock in her size. With the wedding only two weeks off, there isn't time to get another one made and delivered. I told Katie she could have any dress we have in stock for half price to help make up for it. I do hope you can find something she'll like."

Tessa's eyes flitted around the shop at the hundreds of bridal gowns adorning the racks and walls. "I hope so, too. Katie is pretty picky. I just wish she could have come here herself."

"I have a feeling you'll do just fine. Why don't you select six or eight gowns you think she will like, and we'll bag them up so you can take them to Katie for her to choose from."

A sigh of relief washed over Tessa. "You'd do that?"

Della nodded. "Of course. I'm so embarrassed that the supplier sent the wrong size gown." She led Tessa to the far wall. "All of these are Katie's size. If you'll excuse me, I'll be back in just a minute. I need to make a quick phone call."

Tessa nodded then stared at the voluminous mass of white satin and crepe. She wanted to cry. How could she possibly select a gown for her daughter? There were so many styles and shapes. She hadn't realized the selection would be this vast.

"How about that one?" a male voice asked from behind her.

Startled by the sound of Mike's voice, she whirled around, nearly knocking over a mannequin. "What are *you* doing here?"

He gave her a broad smile. "Katie sent me. She thought you could use some help."

"From you?"

The lines around his eyes crinkled as he gave her a second broad smile. "Sure! Why not? I've been to a couple of weddings in my time. How hard can it be to pick out a wedding dress?"

"You'd be surprised. Are you sure you can spare the time? How will the San Diego Police Department get along without you?"

The corners of his mouth turned up as he shrugged. "I guess they'll have to struggle along as best they can. I've told them not to call me unless it's an emergency."

"As if that would stop them." She gave him a look of irritation. "As I recall, everything that happens, even when you are supposed to be off duty, is an emergency."

He raised a brow. "Your fangs are showing, Tessie."

She ignored his remark and didn't respond, although a snappy comeback was on the tip of her tongue.

He pointed to the mannequin she'd nearly toppled. "How about that dress?"

Appalled by his suggestion, she gave him a blank stare. "That one would never do!"

"Why? It's white and has some of those bead things on it. I think she'd like it."

"Mike! That's a long-sleeved sheath. Katie wants a strapless one with a full, flowing skirt and a long train."

"Strapless? Won't that be uncomfortable? How'll she keep it up?"

Tessa rolled her eyes. "Strapless wedding dresses typically have plastic or metal staves in them that hold the bodice in place. They're quite comfortable."

He gestured toward the wall of dresses. "So let's find a good one." Selecting a hanger from the rod, he pulled out a strapless gown with a heavily pleated bodice and skirt. "I'll bet she'd like this one."

"I don't think so. Too much fabric around the bustline and through the hips."

"It's got a long skirt."

"But the skirt is pleated. Katie wants an A-line."

Mike gave her a puzzled look. "A line of what? Those bead things?"

"The term A-line refers to the shape of the skirt, Mr. Garrett," Della inserted as she returned.

He placed the hanger back on the rod. "Whatcha think of this one, Tessie?"

She cringed as he pulled another dress from the rack, this one made with a heavy layer of tulle covering the skirt. "Too fussy. Katie would never go for it."

"Here's a nice one." Della pulled another gown from the selection and splayed the skirt out over a chair. "This is a beautiful dress, much prettier on than it looks on the hanger. The low-cut back is especially nice." She sized Tessa up. "Why don't you try it on, Mrs. Garrett? You and Katie are about the same size."

Tessa held her palm up between them. "No, I don't think so."

"Aw, come on, Tessie—try it on. Let's see what it looks like. You still got a good-lookin' figure."

"Yes, Mrs. Garrett, do try it on."

As Tessa took a closer look at the gown, she decided it was lovely, and more like what she thought Katie would want than any she'd seen so far. "I guess I could—"

Mike moved to one of the rose-colored slipper chairs and seated himself. "I'll wait right here 'til you come out."

She allowed Della to lead her to the fitting room and once she was alone slipped off her jeans and shirt and wiggled into the dress, letting out a little gasp as she peered at the image staring back at her in the mirror. The gown fit her perfectly, and Della was right. It did look much better on than it did on the hanger.

Della tapped gently on the door. "Could you come out, please? Mr. Garrett would like to see the dress on you."

Tessa stared into the mirror. Mike wanted to see her in the dress? The man who all too often wore navy socks with his black suit had suddenly turned into a fashion guru?

"It's much easier to see the dress in the large three-way mirrors in the showroom," Della added. "The back of that gown is so beautiful. You really need to see it in those big mirrors to get the full effect."

Tessa twisted from one side to the other, trying, without success, to see the back of the gown. It was impossible, with the small size of the dressing room, to see the entire back view. She pushed the door open a bit and said to Della, "I'd feel a little foolish strutting around out there in a wedding gown at my age."

"That's not a problem. Right now, you're the only customers in the store. No one, other than my employees and your husband, will see you. Besides, I'll bet you look beautiful in that gown. Times have changed. Although we recommend a pastel color, you'd be surprised how many older women come in and purchase a white gown for their second, or even third, wedding."

Tessa gathered up the train in her arms and moved warily

through the door. "Times have changed. I always thought white was for your first marriage. Isn't it supposed to be a symbol of purity?"

Della grabbed onto the train and gestured toward the showroom. "I always thought so. But with so many couples living together before marriage, to most, it no longer matters."

"I know what you mean. Mike and I hated that Katie and Jim were living together. We've never approved."

"I was impressed when Katie told me Jim had moved out of their condo until after the wedding. Talk about living your values as a new Christian," Della said.

"I agree," Mike chimed in, rising as the two women approached him. "Our daughter and Jim are clearly devoted to one another and their Christian values. I expect those two will be together until death do they part."

Tessa bit her tongue, fearing he was going to elaborate and mention that a certain Christian couple, though they had married *before* living together and the bride had worn the traditional white, had not stayed together as they'd vowed to do. But he didn't. She wondered just how much Katie had told Della and her husband about the details of their breakup.

Della nodded as she lowered Tessa's train to the floor and stooped to arrange it around her feet. "I'm so glad to hear that, Mr. Garrett. It sounds like you approve of Jim for a husband."

"Jim? You bet I approve of him. He's a fine young man, and he loves my daughter. He's going to make a great husband." He nodded toward Tessa. "Even Tessie approves."

The woman rose. "Well, what do you think, Mr. Garrett? Will Katie like this one?"

Tessa felt herself blushing as Mike stood back, squinted, and sized her up from head to toe.

"She'd be nuts not to, if she looks anything like Tessie in that dress."

Della turned toward Tessa with a giggle. "What a sweet husband you have, Mrs. Garrett."

"Oh, he's a sweetie all right," Tessa answered, trying to keep any sarcasm from her voice. She turned her attention to another gown, this one with a heavily beaded lace bodice.

"Oh, you've chosen one of my favorites." Della moved aside the other dresses and pulled the gown from the rack. "This one is so feminine."

Mike smiled his approval. "Put it on, Tessie."

Tessa stepped back, appraising the dress with a frown. "You don't think it's a bit overdone? There are a lot of beads."

"The one Katie selected had a lot of beads," the stylishly dressed young woman reminded her.

"True, and it is beautiful. I like the self-piping at the top of the bodice." Nodding her approval to Della, she headed toward the fitting room.

A few minutes later, she appeared again before Mike. "I do like it. What do you think? This one is a lot like the one Katie had wanted."

His eyes widened. "I'd say it's a keeper. Let's take it to show Katie."

She bobbed her head, unable to mask her smile of approval. "It's my choice. I can visualize Katie in this dress, but we decided on taking six dresses. Let's find at least two or three more."

One hour and eight dresses later, they had selected five dresses to present to their daughter.

"Hey," Mike said as he leaped from the chair and headed toward a mannequin near the front of the store. "What about this one?"

Spinning around, Della gave him a smile. "Good choice, Mr. Garrett! That one came in yesterday. I'd forgotten all about it. Other than the one on the mannequin, we haven't even had a chance to check the others in yet and bring them to the sales floor. I'll go to the stockroom and see if we have it in Katie's size."

The two waited silently for her return.

"We have it," she announced victoriously when she re-appeared. "You must try this one on, Mrs. Garrett. It's going to look fabulous on you."

Mike nodded with enthusiasm. "Yeah, Tessie, try it on. I wanna see you in it."

When she emerged from the fitting room, he rose to his feet with a whistle of approval. "Now that's a dress. Let's buy it!"

Her jaw dropping, Tessa blinked at him. "Without Katie seeing it?"

Smiling, his eyes locked with hers. He stood and moved toward her, the expression he wore looking more like that of the Mike she'd loved and married. A chill ran down her spine causing an involuntary tremble as he took her hand in his and gave it a squeeze. "Tessie, you're beautiful."

"Oh—I—you—" She found herself blubbering like a fool.

"You are," he continued, his thumb gently rotating across her knuckles. "You're as pretty as you were on our wedding day."

Della nodded in agreement. "You do look lovely in that gown. It fits as though it were made for you."

Tessa felt a flush rise to her cheeks. "Thank you for the compliments, but the question is—how will it look on Katie? She's the bride. Not me."

"If Katie looks half as good as you in that dress, Jim will go berserk!"

"Mike!"

"I mean it. We guys like our women to look like women. All I can say is wow!"

"I guess we'll take this dress along with the others for Katie to see," Tessa told her, struggling to keep her voice under control. Mike's freely given, unsolicited compliments had unnerved her. He hadn't given her a compliment like that since long before they had separated.

"Six gowns are going to be hard to handle. Would you like us to deliver them to Katie's condo?"

"We'd really like to take them with us," Tessa told her, remembering the short time until the wedding. "I have a minivan. I can lower the seats, and we can lay the garment bags on the carpeted floor. I'd really like to get them to Katie as soon as possible. She's so anxious to get this thing settled."

Mike gave a snort. "Yeah, Della, that mistake with the gown size really sent her into a tizzy. You should have heard her yell. I thought she was going to bust a gasket."

"I feel awful about that. I'll do whatever I can to make things right for Katie. Of all the people it could have happened to, it *had* to be one of my best friends! Unbelievable. Anyway, we'll have these gowns bagged in no time, Mrs. Garrett, and I'll have someone load them into your van."

Mike stuck out his hand. "Give me your keys, Tessie. I'll go on out and lower the seats."

She pulled them from her purse and handed them to him.

"Be back in a flash."

By the time she had taken off the final gown and handed it to Della, redressed, and run a brush through her hair, they were finished placing all but the last garment bag in her car. "Thanks," she told the helpful woman. "We'll get these back to you as soon as Katie makes a decision."

Della placed the final bag on top of the others and lowered

the door. "If for any reason she doesn't like any of these, I'll be happy to help you select others."

Mike shook his head confidently. "I can tell you right now, she's gonna choose that last one."

"Thanks for your help, Mike," Tessa told him sincerely after Della said good-bye and disappeared through the shop's door. What she'd expected to be a real ordeal had actually been fairly pleasant. It was obvious Mike had been on his best behavior. "I'll let you know which one Katie selects."

He gave his head a vigorous shake. "Hey, no, you don't. I'm going with you!"

"Can you spare that much time?"

"I told you I'm taking some time off. People do that you know."

She slid into the driver's seat and rolled down the window. "I suppose I should be impressed that you spent the last hour or so with me and no one from the SDPD called you."

"Impressed? No, but you might give me a little credit here. This is my daughter's wedding, too. I want to be there for her."

"Isn't it a little late to start being there for her?" Tessa shoved the key in the ignition and gave it a twist. "Where were you all those years when your daughter was growing up?"

"Is that a rhetorical question?"

She yanked the gearshift into DRIVE and revved up the engine. "Call it whatever you like. I'll see you at Katie's." With that, she drove off, leaving him standing in the shop's parking lot staring at her rear bumper.

Mike arrived just seconds after Tessa's car pulled into the parking area in front of Katie and Jim's condo. By the time she reached the minivan's rear door he was matching her stride for stride. Each gathered up three puffy garment bags and headed for the front door.

Jim pulled open the door before they could knock. "Katie's on the sofa waiting for you. I stopped by for an early lunch and to check on her."

"How's she feeling?" Tessa asked, pushing past him and into the comfortable, eclectically decorated room.

"She says fine, but I can tell she's hurting."

From her place on the sofa, Katie gave both her father and mother a teasing smile. "The two of you arriving together? That's a switch!"

"We've brought six beautiful gowns for you to try on," Tessa said, laying her garment bags on a chair and refusing to respond to her daughter's prodding question. "Della said we could bring more if you didn't find one in this group that you liked. She also said you could keep these until you felt like trying them on."

"But I know which one you're gonna pick," Mike told Katie as he placed his garment bags over a second chair.

Grinning, Katie splayed her flattened palm across her chest. "Daddy! You surprise me. I didn't think you'd be able to tell one gown from another."

"Hey, give me a little credit. I watch TV. I read the newspapers. Wait'll you see it. You'll look every bit as good in it as your mom did when she tried it on at the shop."

Katie's eyes sparkled. "You tried it on?"

"She tried on all six of them, and a couple of others, too."

Tessa felt the flush rise to her cheeks again. "It was Della's idea."

"We had to talk her into it," Mike confessed, grabbing Tessa's arm and giving it a squeeze.

"That's so sweet, Mom. I never expected you to do try them on, but we are the same size. What a great idea. Will you model them for me?"

Before she could answer, Mike did. "Sure she will."

Though upset by the fact that he answered for her, with a mother's concern, Tessa placed a hand on her daughter's forehead. "You look great, but are you sure you're up to all of this?"

Katie lovingly tugged her hand away. "Mom, are you kidding me? Other than having a broken ankle and being a bit uncomfortable, I'm fine. I haven't even taken any pain pills since four this morning." She motioned toward their bedroom. "Please put the gowns on so I can see them. I really want to get a decision made."

She turned toward Jim. "Sorry, sweetie, but this would be a good time for you to go back to work. Grooms aren't supposed to see the bridal gown until the bride walks down the aisle."

"I really hate to leave, but I understand. I'll just pick up a sandwich for lunch on the way." Jim stood still, as if unable to move.

Mike sat down on the sofa beside Katie. "You might as well give up and go back to work, Jim. You know how women are about those things."

After picking up his cell phone and car keys from the table, Jim kissed Katie, shook hands with Mike, and kissed Tessa on the cheek. "Call me if you need me."

"Put my favorite on last," Mike instructed Tessa once Jim had closed the door behind him.

Tessa nodded then gathered up the garment bags and headed for the bedroom. Since she'd decided to put them on in the same order she'd done at the store, Mike's selection would have been last anyway, so she decided to let him have his way.

Katie leaned back against the sofa's cushion with an appreciative sigh as Tessa entered wearing the first gown, the one with the low-cut back. "Oh, Mother, I'd never considered that style, but it's beautiful."

Tessa took a slow turn in front of her daughter. "You don't

think the back is too low?"

"Not too low for me," Mike said, eyeing Tessa carefully.

"I was asking Katie."

"I like it." Katie motioned for her mother to take another slow turn. "It looks fabulous on you, Mom."

"Wait'll you see mine. It's even better."

Tessa couldn't help laughing. Much to her surprise, Mike was really getting into this thing.

Katie let out a giggle. "Daddy! I've never seen you like this."

"No one has ever asked me to help select a wedding dress before!"

Tessa did another slow spin for Katie before retreating to the bedroom to don the next dress, the heavily beaded one with the piping along the bodice. *Her* personal choice.

"Umm, I don't know which one I like best," Katie said when her mother appeared in the doorway. "This one is pretty, too, and I love the unusual beading."

"This one is my favorite." Tessa ran her fingers over the beads, noticing their delicate design and sparkle. "I can just see you walking down the aisle in this one."

Mike shook his head. "It's pretty, but not as pretty as mine."

"I do like it, Mom."

He adjusted his position on the sofa's edge, giving his daughter a bit more room. "I like this one, too, but my selection is much better."

Katie tilted her head, first this way then that. "The one Mom has on now may be the wedding gown for me. She looks great in it. I may not even need to see the others. This one would be the perfect substitute for the one I'd picked out."

"She does look great, but wait until you see her in my dress."

Katie let out a giggle. "Your dress, Daddy?"

"He put a claim on it the minute he saw it on the mannequin,"

Tessa explained, ready to retreat to the bedroom for the next change. "You should have seen him going through those racks of dresses."

Tessa appeared three more times, with Katie oohing and aahing over each gown.

"You guys did a wonderful job selecting these dresses. I couldn't have done better myself. They look so different on Mom than they did hanging on those impersonal hangers. Now I don't know which one I like best. Any one of them would do, especially since I'm not able to have the one I really wanted. But I think the beaded bodice one is my favorite. The one Mom likes."

"She's not through yet," Mike reminded her. "There's one more. Mine." He nodded toward Tessa. "Go put it on, Tessie, and pull your hair up on top your head like I like it."

Tessa stared at her husband in disbelief. He remembered how he liked her hair? After all these years? He'd rarely mentioned her hairstyle to her. Even when she'd had it cut.

Mike gave her a gentle smile. "You look good with your hair up like that."

Tessa fingered the hair at the nape of her neck. "Uh—thank you, Mike. You—you never told me."

"If I didn't, I should have." His expression sobered. "I should have told you a lot of things, Tessie—complimented you more. I know that—now that it's too late."

She turned toward the bedroom, blinking back tears. The last thing she wanted was to let Mike see that his words had touched her so deeply. Despite the scoundrel she thought him to be, she still loved him. She always would, no matter how much she denied it to herself.

"Now for the very best one of all," Mike told his daughter, his face aglow when Tessa entered the room, her hair swept up on top of her head as he had requested. "I present my wife, one of the loveliest women I've ever met, wearing my dress."

Katie turned and let out a gasp. "Oh, Mama, Daddy was right! This is the best dress of all. And you are so beautiful in it!"

"She's right, babe." Mike rose and strode toward Tessa, taking her hand and enfolding it in his. "You *are* beautiful!"

Tessa struggled against the tears that filled her eyes to overflowing. For the first time in a long time, she actually felt beautiful. *Oh, God,* her heart cried out. *I love these two people more than life itself. Why, oh why, did our marriage have to fall apart? All I ever wanted out of life was to be a wife and mother, and serve You. Where did I go wrong?*

"That's it, Mother," Katie said in a mere whisper as she motioned her mother to come closer and reached out to touch the soft, satiny white crepe. "That's my wedding gown."

"See, I told you so!" Mike sat back down beside his daughter, smiling a victory smile. "I knew Katie would like this one best."

"It appears you were right," Tessa conceded, a little chafed and wishing Katie would have picked her choice, the one with the heavily beaded bodice, instead of Mike's. "Good thing you like it since as the father of the bride you'll be paying for it. Have you checked the price tag?"

He shrugged. "Nope. How much is it? Two hundred? Three hundred?"

Tessa fished the tag from inside the bodice, grimaced, and then bent close to Mike so he could see it, too.

"Twelve hundred dollars!" he shouted, his eyes bugging out as he peered at the tag. "What's that thing made of? Spun gold?"

"Don't blow a gasket, Daddy." Katie patted his arm. "Remember, Della said she's giving it to me for half price since the supplier goofed up my order. That's only six hundred dollars."

"*Only* six hundred dollars? I had no idea wedding dresses cost that much!"

Katie's face fell. "Maybe we could find a cheaper one."

"Well, this is just dandy!" Her hands on her hips, Tessa glared at him. "Mike Garrett! This is your daughter's wedding gown we're talking about—for a once in a lifetime event. I hope you're not going to do this with every thing for the wedding. Nothing is cheap, believe me. I've helped with dozens of weddings at the church. Sometimes people even have to take out a mortgage on their home to pay for their children's weddings."

Katie brushed a tear from her cheek and sniffled, obviously upset by her father's words. "It's okay, Mom. I don't want to throw Daddy into debt. I've got a little money set aside to buy a new car in the spring. I'll pay for my wedding gown."

Mike stood and began to fiddle with the change in his pocket. "No, you won't. Your mother is right. This wedding is important. I'm sorry for complaining. I shouldn't have said anything. It's just that I never expected it would cost so much. Go ahead with your plans, okay? I don't want to throw a wet blanket on things."

"I'm really surprised at you, Mike," Tessa flung out at him. "As long as you've worked for the San Diego PD you should be making some pretty good money. I can't believe you're being such a cheapskate about this."

His fist came down on a nearby desk with a thud. "I'm not being a cheapskate! I'm only being practical. Where do you think all that *good* money you're talking about is going? I'll tell you where it's going. It's going to pay the mortgage for the house you live in. It pays your utility bills, the groceries in your cupboard, the insurance on your car, and the clothing on your back. How many men do you know whose wife kicked them out of the house would continue to pay the bills like I have? Not many, I can assure you. But I promised God the day I married you, Tessie Garrett, I would provide for you and take care of you, for better *and* for worse. These past eight years have been for the worse, but I've hung in there. I also have to pay to keep a roof over my own head. I live in a tiny one-bedroom apartment, drive a five-year-old car, and often fix myself a bowl of soup in the microwave and call it a meal, just to keep you in the lifestyle you deserve. Does that give you an idea where my *good* money goes?"

Katie covered her face with her hands and began to sob. "I'm sorry. I never m—meant to cause all this trouble. For—forget about the dress. Forget about the w—wedding. Jim and I will elope."

Mike reached his arm toward his daughter, but Tessa pushed her way in between him and Katie, wedging her body between the two of them. "Don't cry, sweetheart." She sent a meaningful glance toward Mike as she wrapped her arms about her precious daughter and pulled her close. "You'll have your wedding—just the way you wanted it. Your father was only letting off steam."

Mike began to pace about the room, nervously running his fingers through his hair. "I'm sorry, Katie, honest I am. I'd like to give you the moon, the stars, and anything else you want. I may not be able to do that, but I *can* give you a decent wedding. I promise I'll try to keep my mouth shut."

Katie lifted watery eyes, her face stained with tears. "I had hoped my wedding would bring you and Mom together, but I've just made things even worse!"

"No, you haven't, honey. Your father and I had a good time at Della's shop, didn't we, Mike?" Tessa shot Mike a warning look, hoping, for Katie's sake, he'd take the hint and agree with her.

"Uh—yeah—we sure did. We even had a few laughs. That hasn't happened in a long time."

"Neither of us wants to upset you, Katie, or have you cancel your wedding plans." Tessa placed a gentle kiss on Katie's cheek. "Now that you've chosen your wedding gown, the rest will be easy. Just tell us what else you want us to do, and your father and I will put our differences aside and get busy on it. Won't we, Mike?"

His face brightened, and he smiled at Tessa. "Yep, we sure will. Your mama and I love you, pumpkin. This is gonna be the best wedding Seaside Community Church as seen in a long time."

Katie winced as she shifted her leg on the ottoman. "You're sure about this? The two of you don't mind working together?"

"For you, my sweet girl, I'll do anything." Tessa sent a questioning glance toward Mike.

"Me, too, honey. Your mother and I used to be a great team. No reason we can't do it again."

Katie dabbed at her eyes with her shirttail. "So the wedding is on?"

Tessa brushed a lock of damp hair from her daughter's face. "The wedding is on."

❧

Tessa sat in her favorite family room chair staring at the TV screen but not hearing a word of the six o'clock news. Her mind was on the events of the day. Who would have ever thought she and Mike would actually offer to work together and promise to get along until after the wedding?

When the doorbell rang a few minutes later, she debated about even answering the door, not in the mood to talk to anyone. Her minivan was in the garage. No one would even know she was there. But when it rang a second, third, and even fourth time, she leaped from the chair and rushed toward the door. Who could be that persistent? "Okay, okay! I'm coming!"

But when she looked out the door's peephole, no one was there. About ready to back away from the door and return to her chair, she decided to take a second look. Though she hadn't noticed it the first time, on the little wrought iron bench she kept on the front porch was a pizza box from the local pizzeria. Had they made a mistake and left the box at the wrong address? Without getting paid? That didn't make any sense—unless the caller paid by phone with their bank or credit card.

Thinking surely that was what had happened, she opened the door, planning to call and tell them they had left it at the wrong house. But when she bent to pick up the box, she heard a familiar voice from behind the hedge near the door.

"Hi." Mike stepped up onto the porch with a boyish smile that made her heart zing. "I hope you haven't eaten. Do you still like sausage and onion pizza?"

Though Mike was the last person she had expected to see at her door, she allowed the corners of her mouth to inch up into a smile. She had promised Katie she was going to get along with Mike. Perhaps now would be a good time to start.

❧

To his surprise, she smiled and motioned him inside. "Sausage and onion *is* still my favorite. I'm surprised you remembered."

"I remember many things about you, Tessie. I think about them sometimes when I'm alone in my apartment or sitting by myself in my car while out on a stakeout." After giving her a sheepish grin, he moved in past her. "I'm sorry for what I said today. It was stupid and uncalled-for. As you know from experience, I'm not famous for keeping my mouth shut."

"You're not the only one. I say things, too—things I'm sorry for later." Tessa followed him into the family room and motioned toward the recliner, the one that had been his. "Sit down. I'll put the pizza on some plates and get us something to drink. Coffee okay? I just made a fresh pot, or would you prefer something cold?"

"Whatever you're having." He started to lower himself into the recliner but stopped midway, bracing himself against the chair's arm. "I could help."

She gestured toward the CD player. "You could put on some nice music."

Mike selected one of the many CDs by Christian artists filed neatly on the shelf then stood glancing about the room as the music began to play. Roses. There were roses everywhere. On the drapery, the pillows on the sofa, in vases on the tables and mantel, on the delicate figurines Tessa collected, everywhere. And there were mirrors, too—beveled mirrors, ornately trimmed mirrors, even mirror-trimmed sconces on the walls.

In no time, she was back.

"Whatcha call this type of decorating? With all the roses and stuff?" he asked after Tessa prayed and thanked the Lord for their food.

She pulled a string of cheese from her chin with a laugh. "Shabby chic."

"Oh, yeah, I remember that crazy decorating term. Wonder who thought that one up? I also remember the trips you and Ellen made to antique stores and flea markets to find all these pieces."

"It's a bit gaudy for some tastes, but I love it. It's warm and homey and inviting."

"I like it, too. Always did." Mike bit into his pizza with

enthusiasm. "This is like old times."

She seemed to weigh her words carefully before speaking. "Yes, it is like old times, but you missed many of those old times—times Katie and I wished you were with us."

He stared off into space, and Tessa seemed suddenly uncomfortable.

"I didn't say that to upset you, Mike. I was simply stating a fact. We did wish you were there with us. You were a part of our family—the head of our family. Our family unit was incomplete without you."

Mike stared at her for a moment then asked, "Do you have any idea how difficult you made it for me, Tessie? I loved my family. Still do. I wanted you to be able to be home with Katie instead of going to work like so many other women were doing. All those extra hours I worked made that possible, yet, instead of thanks, all I received from you was criticism."

She wore a look of frustration. "I would rather have gone to work part-time and had you home! Didn't you realize that?"

"But you preferred to be a stay-at-home mom, didn't you?"

"Not at the risk of losing you! I wanted to be with you! I needed to be with you!"

"Then why were you always so angry?"

"Me angry? You were the one who was always angry! Not me!"

"Only after you lit into me for being late or missing supper! You never seemed to realize I wasn't gone by choice. It was my job!"

Tessa visibly bristled. Jumping to her feet, she leaned over him, her face blanketed with hurt, her finger jabbing at her chest. "A job for you maybe but I was the one waiting at home for you, praying to God that you were safe! And you call me angry?"

He grabbed her wrist and glared at her as she leaned over him, his face so close she could feel his hot breath on her cheeks. "I loved you, Mike. You were everything to me, and you rejected me."

His grip lessened some, but he continued to keep her imprisoned in his grasp. "Didn't you know I loved you, too?"

"I used to think you did, but then I began to wonder. You quit holding me, kissing me—paying any attention to me at all."

"I didn't think you wanted me to kiss you."

"I did. I wanted—"

Before she could finish her sentence, he tugged her to him and, taking her in his arms and pulling her onto his lap, he kissed her tenderly, passionately, like he'd kissed her the first year of their marriage.

Tessa wanted to pull away, but she couldn't. Her lips wouldn't allow it. It was as if she and Mike had suddenly been transported back twenty-some years, to a time when they couldn't keep their hands off each other. When each did everything they could to please the other. She tried to stop her hands when they moved to cradle the back of his neck, and her fingers as they twined themselves in the hair at his nape, but they wouldn't obey.

"This is where you belong, Tessie," he murmured against her willing lips. "Here in my arms."

Waves of pleasure swept over her as she leaned into him.

"You're my wife, Tessie," he whispered, nuzzling his chin in her hair. "This is where God intended you to be."

Tessa shifted in his arms as reality struck. Other than the two of them having a few good times as they'd worked on Katie's wedding, nothing had changed. Mike was still Mike the cop. Mike, the man who always put his work above all else in his life. The man who cared little about the time he spent away from his family or the danger he faced every day. Needing to free herself from his grasp, Tessa placed her hands on his chest and pushed away. "I may have belonged in your arms once, but not now. The only thing that has changed between us, Mike, is that we've grown older and probably each more set in our ways. While I don't like living alone, I've resigned myself to it, and I'm doing quite nicely. And yes, I'm sure God wanted us to be together but apparently the only way you wanted us to be together was on your terms. Not His."

With a grunt of exasperation, Mike stood and gave his head a shake. "Maybe I'd better go."

Working hard at keeping her tears at bay, she turned her face away from him. "That's probably a very good idea."

Mike grabbed the remaining slice of pizza from his plate and, without looking back or saying another word, moved quickly through the house and out the front door. It slammed hard behind him, leaving Tessa brokenhearted and dreading her next meeting with him.

five

That woman!" Mike shouted into the air as he slammed the car door and rammed the key into the ignition.

He shoved the pizza into his mouth, yanked the gearshift into reverse, and hit the accelerator, his tires squealing as the car backed into the street. "How can one woman claim to be a Christian and be so cantankerous?" he mumbled, his mouth still busy with the pizza. He pounded his fist on the steering wheel.

Why is it you never see her side of things? a still, small voice said from deep within his heart.

"Her side of things? What does she expect from me? I'm only a few years from retirement. Does she want me to quit my job? I'm too old to start over. If she's the wonderful Christian everyone thinks she is, why doesn't she understand my needs?"

Your needs? What are your needs, Mike? The biggest need in your life is Me. Think about it. You've quit attending church. You quit praying. You quit fellowshipping with Me. How long has it been since you've prayed? Come to Me with your problems, instead of either ignoring them or trying to handle them yourself.

"I had to work Sundays, God. You know that. I'm a San Diego police detective. Working Sundays was part of my job."

You volunteered to work most of those Sundays. Are you sure the demands of your job weren't simply convenient excuses to avoid attending church?

Mike let out a sigh. "Like I've always told Tessie, the bad guys don't take Sundays off. They work seven days a week."

Couldn't another detective, perhaps one who didn't claim My name and didn't have a family who needed him, work on Sunday?

Though Mike tried to come up with a viable answer, he couldn't. It *had* been his choice to work on Sundays. Oh, not at first. The first few times he'd done it, it had been because of the high profile case he'd been working on. He'd been so close to solving it that every hour he'd spent on it had been necessary, even the hours he'd worked on Sunday. Because of his hard work and meticulous attention to detail, a hardened criminal who'd been frightening the entire city had been captured, prosecuted, and was serving time behind bars. Mike had fully intended to get back into his regular church-attending routine once that case was settled, but it hadn't happened. Another important case needed his attention, and the rest was history.

To his relief, a call coming through on the police scanner broke into his thoughts and caught his attention, taking away the feelings of guilt that constantly plagued him. Within seconds he was off and running, adrenaline flowing through his veins like a healing salve, heading to assist Brad Turner, the other detective, who'd just uncovered some new evidence in a case the two of them were working on.

Forgotten and pushed into the recesses of his mind, the still small voice again became silent.

&

Sleep eluded Tessa most of the night, not because of what Mike had said, but because of her attitude and the words she had allowed to escape her own mouth.

By five thirty, she was up, dressed, and working out her frustrations in the flowerbeds.

By eight, she had cleaned out the refrigerator, mopped the kitchen floor, run a load of laundry, and vacuumed the family room, none of which needed to be done.

By eight thirty, she was sitting at her desk, staring at the phone, wondering if it was too early to call Katie. Deciding to risk waking her she reached for the phone, only to have it ring as she touched it.

"Hi, Mom. I know you were concerned about the gowns being returned. I phoned the shop a few minutes ago, and Della said she'd send the truck to pick them up later today. Oh, by the way, other than hating to spend my days on this couch, I'm fine. Don't worry about me. My ankle barely hurts now."

Tessa smiled into the phone. "I was just about to call you. I'm glad you're feeling better and that the return of the gowns has been taken care of. Now—what do you want me to do next?"

"I kinda hate to ask."

"Ask away. I said I'd help in any way I could."

There was a pause on the other end. "Dad called a little while ago to see how I was. I told him I really needed him to go with Jim to select the tuxedos the guys will be renting."

Tessa let out a snicker. "And you want me to go along, to make sure they don't pick out something that will embarrass you, right?"

There was a giggle on the other end. "I knew you'd understand, Mom. Do you mind going? They're meeting Jordan, Nathan, and Brandon there at ten."

"Of course I don't mind, sweetie. Anything else?"

"I think I can trust Della, Valene, and Vanessa to pick out their dresses and one for little Carrie, so you don't need to bother with those, but you'll need to decide on your own dress as soon as you can."

"Sure, honey. Got any suggestions?"

"I was thinking of something in a very pale green for you, almost to the pastel shade, full-length, and maybe in a soft, flowing crepe. Whatcha think?"

"I think it sounds perfect, but with the wedding being only two weeks away, you'd better give me a backup color choice in case I can't find a green one."

"If you can't find green, how about ivory?"

"Whatever you say. I'll stop by Della's shop tomorrow. I'm sure she'll have the perfect dress. Now, I'd better hustle if I'm going to get to the formal wear place by ten. I'll call you later."

Tessa was already in the store, waiting, when Mike and the other men entered. They were so caught up in a conversation about a football quarterback who had just signed a multimillion-dollar contract that they didn't even notice her.

Mike spun around at the sound of her voice. "What are you doing here?"

Tessa closed the magazine she'd been idly scanning and rose to join them. "Katie mentioned you men were selecting your tuxedos this morning. I thought perhaps I could help."

He gave her a puzzled look. "Help with what? There's nothing to help with. A tuxedo is a tuxedo, isn't it? Black and boring."

The salesman, overhearing their conversation, stepped in. "Oh, no, sir. Not anymore it isn't. These days, tuxedos come in all colors and dozens of styles. You name it, we have it."

Jim gestured toward a mannequin. "How about something like that, Mike?"

Mike crinkled up his face. "Too fancy for me. I think we should stick with something plainer. That looks kinda sissy-like."

"The last wedding Valene and I attended," Jordan said, "the men all wore that off-white color. It looked pretty good."

Mike gave his head a shake. "Off-white? That'd get dirty too quick."

Nathan and Brandon chortled.

"You're only going to wear it once, Mike," Nathan said.

Jim nodded. "From what Katie said, I think she'd prefer we go with the off-white. She'd suggested off-white shirts, too."

"What color ties and cummerbunds?" Jordan asked, fingering a heavily pleated-front shirt on the display rack.

Jim frowned. "If Katie had a preference on that one, I don't remember."

Tessa was trying her best to keep out of the conversation, but Katie had specifically mentioned having the men go with a monochromatic theme. "Off-white. Katie told me she wanted everything off-white."

"Do you prefer the traditional length jackets, or perhaps the wonderful new longer length?" the clerk asked, sizing up the five men. "The longer length is complimentary to any man's build."

Grinning, Mike glanced at his companions then patted his stomach. "I guess he means me."

"I like the longer length," Jim said with a patronizing smile. "I think Katie would, too."

Tessa wanted to voice her approval but decided to stay out of it, rather than risk letting Mike think she was taking over in an area that should be left to him.

"This one is nice." The salesman pulled a hanger from the rack and proudly held out a longer-length, off-white tuxedo. "How about something like this?"

The five nodded their approval.

"Now that the color and style has been decided upon, let's select your shoes, and you can try them with the tuxedos, to get a better idea of the whole picture," the man suggested, gesturing to the wall of shoe boxes at the side of the salesroom.

Mike shook his head. "We don't need shoes. We'll wear our own."

The man stopped in his tracks, turned, and stared at Mike. "You are joking, sir, aren't you?"

Seeming mystified, Mike frowned. "No, I'm not joking. We each own perfectly good shoes, and wearing our own will be a lot more comfortable than breaking in a new pair. He turned to his companions. "You each have a pair of black shoes, don't you?"

Brandon burst out laughing. "Good one, Mike! You almost had me believing you were serious."

Jim gave him a warning frown. "I think Mike was serious, Brandon."

Tessa could stand it no longer. "Mike, you can't wear black shoes with off-white tuxedos!"

His gaze locked with hers. "Why not? No one is going to be looking at our feet. They'll all be looking at Katie."

Convinced this was the reason Katie had suggested she tag along, Tessa took charge but tried to keep her voice soft. "Mike, this is your daughter's wedding. She wants the men to wear off-white tuxedos with off-white shirts, ties, and cummerbunds, and shoes that will complement the look. I think you'd better go with whichever shoes the salesman suggests."

After much discussion and finally agreeing on the shoes to be worn, the group moved to the shirt area.

"The ruffled front shirts. Definitely, you'll want the ruffled front shirts." The salesman pointed to a display model. "This shirt is perfect with the tuxedos you've selected. They're a bit more expensive, but well worth it."

Screwing up his face and holding his hands up between his companions and himself, Mike backed away. "Me? Wear a ruffled shirt? Forget it!"

"I don't know about that, Mike. I think Katie would prefer the ruffled shirts," Jim countered meekly, sounding as though he was afraid to cross his future father-in-law. "I heard her talking about them."

Mike gave Jim a shrug and expression of surrender. "Okay! I acquiesce. Whatever Katie wants is what I want, too."

Tessa busied herself in the waiting area while the men tried on their outfits, impatiently looking at more of the store's magazines until the five appeared, each looking more handsome than she could have imagined. She clapped her hands and smiled her approval. "Bravo! You guys look great! Katie will be so pleased."

Mike gave her a half smile as he smoothed at his lapels. "You really think so? We don't look dumb in these frilly shirts?"

She returned his smile. "You all look terribly handsome."

He turned to the clerk. "So, are we all through here? That's it?"

The man nodded. "Yes, sir, that's it. As soon as the tailor marks the length of your trousers and sleeves and you get redressed, I'll have your statement ready. Of course, you'll want to put down a deposit."

"Sure, just let me know how much it is, and I'll write you a check," Mike called back over his shoulder as he headed for the fitting room, much to Tessa's surprise.

He's certainly had a change of heart, she thought as she moved back to her seat. *Maybe our little talk did some good. I hope he's prepared for what this is going to cost him.*

Mike returned twenty minutes later, checkbook in hand, and walked up to the checkout counter. "Hey, that tailor guy of yours sure knows his stuff," he told the salesman. "He took my measurements and got me outta there in a flash. Got my bill ready?"

The clerk nodded, handed him the sales slip, and pointed to a figure near the bottom. "This is your total, sir, and this is the deposit we'll need from you today. You can pay the remainder when you pick up your garments."

Mike gave Tessa a smile she interpreted as cocky, as if to say he had resigned himself to whatever the wedding was going to cost him.

Then he looked at the bill.

"What? This much? I didn't want to *buy* those tuxes. I thought we were only going to rent them!"

"Those *are* the rental prices, sir," the clerk responded quickly, pointing to the totals. "If you were buying them, the cost would be much higher, I can assure you. I think you'll find our rates favorably comparable with those of the other shops in town."

His face flushed, Mike turned quickly to Tessa. "I told you we should wear our own shoes. Did you see what those things cost? And we aren't even buying them! And I sure don't need to be paying extra for ruffles on my shirt!"

She hurried to his side and patted his arm gently, hoping to calm him down before Jim and the others returned from their fittings. "I'm sorry, Mike. I know this is a lot of money but there's no way to avoid it. You do want Katie to have a formal wedding, don't you? The kind of wedding she deserves?"

He ran his fingers through his graying temples. "You know I do, Tessie, but somehow we have to keep a handle on this. I'm a cop, living on a cop's pay. As much as I'd like to give Katie carte blanche, I have to be realistic. I'm still paying on her last year's college bill."

She knew what he was saying was true. Several months ago, Katie had mentioned to her that she and Jim were planning on taking over the loan Mike had gotten from the bank to get Katie through college. They'd even told Mike of their plans, but he wouldn't hear of it. He'd said it was not only his responsibility to make sure Katie could finish college, but also his pleasure and joy to do so.

Tessa placed a comforting hand on his shoulder. "Don't

worry about it, Mike. I'll help you look for ways to cut down on the costs of the other things."

"We do have a finance plan, should you desire to use it," the clerk volunteered. "Many people take advantage of this service."

Mike shook his head. "Nope, I'll pay for the entire amount now."

"But, Mike—"

He held up a hand to silence her. "It'll be fine. I'll put everything else on my credit card."

"But if you don't pay those off monthly, the interest really builds up!"

The expression on his face softening, Mike took her hand in his and gave it a pat. "Let me worry about it, Tessie girl. You just keep your mind on giving our Katie the best wedding ever, okay?"

"But—"

His forefinger touched her lips, cutting her off. "No more. I mean it, Tessie. I've shot my mouth off more now than I should have. Please don't tell Katie. With that broken ankle and a wedding not quite two weeks off, she has enough on her plate right now. If you're gonna talk to anyone about it, talk to the Lord. Tell Him I need help."

You do need help, Mike, but not only in your finances. You need Him to touch your heart and bring you back to Him. I—I need His touch, too. Though I try, I can't forgive you for what you've done to me and to our family.

Jim came out of the fitting room area with Jordan, Nathan, and Brandon following close behind. "Hey, Dad," he called out to Mike, "got everything taken care of?"

Mike turned long enough to wink at Tessa. That was the first time Jim had referred to him as Dad. "Everything is under control."

"How'd it go, Mom?" Katie asked Tessa when she stopped by her condo an hour later. "Did Daddy behave himself?"

Tessa smiled as the morning's events rushed through her mind. "They went okay. You should've seen how handsome your father and the others looked. I really think you're going to be pleased with the tuxedos and other things they chose."

Katie leaned forward and gave her arm a playful jab. "*They* chose, or *you* chose?"

"I guess you could say we all picked them out together."

"Has Daddy seen the bill yet?"

"Yes, he saw it."

"Did he come unglued or go into shock?"

Remembering Mike's request that he not tell Katie his initial reaction, Tessa chose her words carefully. "He was a little startled at first, but he did quite well once the initial shock wore off. You would have been proud of him."

Katie leaned back in the cushions surrounding her on the sofa and rubbed at her temples. "Jim and I hate it that Daddy is going to pay for our wedding. We know he can't afford it."

"It's traditional for the bride's parents to pay for the wedding. I'm sure your father wouldn't have it any other way."

"Mom, he's still paying on my college bill! I can't expect the man to do everything! Jim is making good money now. It just doesn't seem fair to put the entire cost on Dad."

"Just this morning, your father told me he wants you to have the best wedding ever. If he didn't mean it, I'm sure he never would have said it." Tessa smiled at Katie. "Now that we have the tuxedos taken care of, what's next?"

Katie tugged on her mother's sleeve. "*Your* dress, Mom. Valene called while you were helping Dad with the tuxedos. She and Vanessa went to Della's bridal salon this morning and selected their dresses and one for my flower girl." Katie paused with a laugh. "It took a little doing. Since Vanessa is about four months pregnant now, they wanted to find a dress that would disguise her slightly bulging abdomen. I'm so excited for them. She and Nathan are going to make wonderful parents. Maybe someday Jim and I will have a baby."

Tessa smiled at the thought. How she'd relished that idea.

"Just think, you and Daddy—grandparents. What would you think about that?"

Her heart swelling with love for this child who might one day become a mother herself, Tessa answered, "I'd love it. I know your father would, too."

Katie let out a wistful sigh. "Someday, Mom, someday. I have to establish myself as a full-fledged architect first. Now back to the wedding. Other than the tux for Ryan—he's going to be such a handsome ring bearer—which is being taken care of this morning, your dress is the only wedding garment left." Katie gave her a mischievous grin. "Want me to get Daddy to go along and help you decide on it?"

Tessa responded with a nervous laugh. "No, thanks. That's one chore I think I can handle all by myself."

"I've seen him giving you the eye lately. I'm sure he'd be more than willing to—"

"Katie! I said no!"

❧

Mike sat in his apartment at his makeshift desk, which was nothing more than a card table with a folding chair, scratching his head while going over his monthly bank statement. "My credit cards are nearly maxed out, and the wedding expenses aren't even added yet. I sure wish that daughter of mine and Jim would have put off their marriage until spring," he told Felix, who wasn't even interested enough to look in his direction. "Maybe by that time I could have had some of these bills paid off."

Letting loose a deep sigh, he leaned back in the chair and locked his hands behind his head, his legs extended beneath the table. "Pride is sure a vengeful thing, Felix. Mine's gotten me in hot water more times than I dare to count."

He closed his eyes and tried to imagine what the past years would have been like if he would have valued his family more and not spent his life being caught up in the pursuit of criminals. His thoughts went to his friend, Bill Zobel, his former accountability partner. How long had it been since the two of them had spent even five minutes together? Up until he'd become so busy with his job, he'd looked to Bill as his role model. Now he barely thought of the man.

At one time, Bill was everything Mike wanted to be. A fine, upstanding Christian, whom men looked up to and admired— a real friend when you needed him, who seemed to sense your need even before you realized it yourself, and a man of prayer. How many times had Bill placed a hand on Mike's shoulder and prayed for him, asking God to have His way in his life? When had the two men begun to part ways?

Searching his heart, Mike had to admit their close friendship had begun to deteriorate when he no longer had time to attend the men's fellowship group at their church. Bill Zobel had phoned him over and over, even come down to his office at the SDPD to try to talk to him, but Mike had become so involved with his excessive caseload he'd barely had time to say more than a pleasant hello. Looking back now, some of Bill's sage advice replayed in his mind.

"Your family needs you," he'd said. *"Are you sure you have to work this many hours? Mike, it's not good for you to miss church. You need to hear God's Word, and you need the fellowship and strength of other believers in your life. Your wife loves you and*

needs you in her life. Mike, you're playing with fire. You're not giving God first place like you used to. He's a jealous God. He wants you to love and worship Him." And his final words the last time the two men were together—*"Mike, you're way off base. You need to get your life in order before it's too late."*

Mike grimaced as he remembered how he'd blown his stack and told the man to stay out of his life and mind his own business. Bill had responded by staring at him, openmouthed, and then walked away. Other than an occasional hello when they met on the street or at the hardware store, though he still greeted him warmly, his friend had done exactly what Mike had told him to do. Stay out of his life. Through his own actions, Mike had lost not only his wife, family, home, and best friend, he'd lost touch with God.

What'd I tell Jim this morning? Everything is under control? Everything is far from under control. And me and my selfish, uncaring attitudes are the reason!

20

Tessa stared at the doorbell. Should she press it? She knew Mike was home. His car was parked at the curb. Maybe she could go on to the caterer by herself. After all, what did Mike know about planning a wedding reception? But he was being such a good sport about paying for everything; shouldn't he be included in any decisions made in regards to the wedding?

Maybe she should go on to the bridal shop and select her dress, but that was one chore that could be put off until later in the day. The most important task now was to make sure the caterer could do the reception on Christmas Day.

She reached toward the doorbell but before she could press it, the door opened and Mike appeared, looking haggard and weary.

"Tessie! I thought I heard a car drive up. What are you doing here?"

"I'm on my way to see the caterer, and I thought you might like to come along." She glanced past him into the dingy room. It was a mess. Worn clothing was draped over furniture. Dirty dishes cluttered the end tables. Empty food wrappers lay scattered on the floor. The place looked like a pigsty, and not at all like Mike had kept things when he had lived at home.

Seeming to note her concern, he stepped out into the hallway, pulling the door partially closed behind him. "I—I'd invite you in, but I've been so busy I haven't had time to tidy the place up, and I know how you hate a messy house."

She forced a slight grin. "I've learned there are other things more important than a meticulously kept house."

"I'd really like to go to the caterer with you. Can you give me a minute? I need to shut down the computer and get my jacket."

"I could meet you there."

He shook his head. "Why don't you let me drive you?"

"It's really not necessary."

"I know, but there's no sense in taking two cars."

Ride around with Mike? She wasn't sure that was a wise idea.

"I promise not to bite."

Not being able to think of a single excuse that wouldn't ignite another argument, she reluctantly agreed.

"Maybe you'll let me take you to dinner afterward." He grinned then moved back into his apartment, closing the door behind him before she could respond.

Tessa stood in the empty hall, waiting, feeling as awkward as she had the first day Mike offered to drive her home from school. In less than two minutes he was back, his hair combed, jacket on, and looking more like himself. She followed him out the building's front door to his car and waited until he opened the door for her, as he'd done so many times before. But one glance at the cluttered interior told her he wasn't any better at keeping his car clean than he was his apartment. Without comment, she pushed a bag of potato chips and an empty pop can onto the floor and climbed in.

"Sorry about the mess," he told her as he slid into the driver's seat.

She shrugged. "No problem."

The traffic was light, and they reached the caterer's shop in less than ten minutes, which left little time for conversation.

"We no can do Christmas Day wedding. No way!" the little man at the shop said in broken English, without even hearing them out.

Undaunted, Mike and Tessa made their way to the second caterer on Katie's list, receiving the same answer. "No!"

The man at the third catering shop took even less time to decline.

"Now what?" Tessa crossed her arms over her chest and stared glumly out the window of Mike's car, blinking back tears of sadness. Katie was depending on them to work things out, and they were failing her. "You can't have a wedding without a rehearsal dinner and a reception. Katie is going to be brokenhearted when we tell her the wedding is going to have to be canceled after all."

Mike circled his arms about the steering wheel, staring straight ahead. "We could always do it ourselves."

Tessa's jaw dropped. "Do the rehearsal dinner and the reception? Surely you're kidding!"

His eyes twinkled. "Think about it, Tessie. You could fix some big pans of your famous lasagna and maybe some of those caramel pies everyone likes. It'd be great! Or maybe we could have pizza delivered to the church."

The man was mad! She'd never be able to do such a ridiculous thing. Besides helping Katie with the wedding, she had Christmas shopping to do.

"We could get some cans of that tropical punch-type stuff to put in that fountain punch bowl for the reception, and we could buy several kinds of cookies from that deli down on the corner."

"And maybe we could use paper plates and napkins, and plastic forks," Tessa added facetiously.

"It'd sure save me a few bucks!"

Tessa couldn't believe her ears. "You're serious."

"Don't you think it'd be better than canceling the wedding?"

"Mike, there is no way we could do such a ridiculous thing! Do you have any idea how much work we're talking about? Not to mention the time it would take. Time we don't have. And it'd be totally inappropriate."

He screwed up his face. "You're probably right. It was a dumb idea, but we can't give up. Is there another caterer on that list?"

She checked the paper then sighed. "One more, but this one is way on the other side of town."

Mike started the engine and pulled out onto the street. "Can't hurt to try."

"You're not giving us much notice," the final caterer on the list said when they explained they wanted him to provide the rehearsal dinner on the evening of the twenty-third. "But we don't want to disappoint your daughter. Sounds like she's had enough trouble already. Since we'll be dealing with a fairly small group, I think we can handle it. Now when is the wedding?"

Chafing from the refusals of the other three, Tessa sent a cautious glance toward Mike then back to the caterer. "Early evening—Christmas Day."

"What? You want us to cater a wedding reception on Christmas Day? Impossible!" the caterer told them excitedly, waving his hands in the air. "I'd have a terrible time pulling a crew together. No one wants to work on Christmas Day!"

Tessa once again explained Katie's broken ankle was what kept her from coming to speak to him herself. "Her father and I"—Tessa gestured toward Mike—"were married on Christmas Day. Katie has her heart set on doing the same thing. We'd really hate to disappoint her."

He appeared a little calmer. "That's an admirable reason. Not many couples stay together as long as apparently you and Mr. Garrett have." Rubbing his chin, the man frowned thoughtfully. "I'd have to charge you more. My employees would expect overtime pay."

Mike tugged at his collar and cleared his throat. "Whatever it takes. I just want to make my daughter happy."

As if in deep thought, the man eyed them both then rose. "Give me a few minutes. Let me talk to my crew."

As soon as he disappeared into the back room, Tessa turned to Mike with concern. "You're already counting pennies. Can you afford to pay the caterer more?"

Mike fingered his chin. "Not really, but I'll manage. Just don't mention it to Katie, okay?"

The man came back before she could respond.

"Believe it or not, when I told them about your daughter's situation, several of my staff members offered to work on Christmas Day. Now tell me what you have in mind."

Both relieved and encouraged by this good news, Tessa pulled Katie's notes from her purse and handed them to him. "This is basically what she had in mind, but she's wide open to suggestion."

He read the notes slowly, nodding, and occasionally jotting

details in the margin, smiling when he reached the end. "My hat's off to your daughter. She's done a good job. I would suggest adding a lovely, fresh green salad to the dinner, and maybe make one of the cakes chocolate instead of vanilla for the reception but, other than that, I like what she's done. Now let's select the tablecloths, punch bowl fountain, and the other things we'll need to make her wedding as spectacular as she'd like. It shouldn't be too difficult. Katie was very specific in her written instructions. She said there would be around twenty at the rehearsal dinner, but she never mentioned how many would be at the wedding." He poised his pen over an order pad.

Tessa gave him a confident smile. "I can answer that one. Since their wedding will be over a holiday, most of their college friends will be home and able to attend. Then, in addition to our neighbors and friends and church members, there'll be a number of family members. We figured between two hundred and two hundred fifty."

Mike turned to stare at her. "That many? I thought this was going to be a small wedding."

"Katie tried to keep the guest list small, Mike, but she simply has to invite certain people," Tessa explained, wishing they would have discussed this in private instead of in front of the caterer.

Looking over the half-glasses perched low on his nose, the man glanced up from his pad. "Two hundred and fifty *is* a small wedding, Mr. Garrett. You should see some of the weddings we cater."

Mike stuck his hands into his pockets, rattling his change. "So what's it gonna cost me?"

The man pulled a small calculator from a nearby shelf and began punching buttons.

Tessa jabbed an elbow into Mike's ribs when he tried to

peer over the man's shoulder.

"Remember I said I would have to charge you more because I'd have to pay my employees overtime," the man said while jotting a few figures on the order pad.

Mike nodded. "Yeah, I remember."

The caterer leaned forward and pointed to the pad. "Here's the total, and of course you'll want to add a generous gratuity."

Tessa thought Mike was going to pass out. His face turned white, and he began to gasp for air.

After shooting a quick glance at Tessa, he sucked in a deep breath. "I—I never dreamed it would be that much! Is there any way we can cut the cost down?"

The man pursed his lips. "I guess we could eliminate the fresh green salad for the rehearsal dinner, but I wouldn't recommend it."

Tessa looped her arm through his. "The green salad would be a nice addition, Mike."

Mike stared at the figures again. "You really think so?"

She nodded. "We could ask Katie to trim the guest list."

"I'd hate to ask her to do that." Mike stared at the floor for a moment then, taking on a faint smile of surrender, told the caterer, "Let's leave the salad in and plan on two hundred fifty guests for the reception. My little girl is getting married. I want things to be right."

"We'll do our best," the man assured him.

"Well, we did it," Mike told Tessa with a shrug and a halfhearted smile as they left the shop. "We actually booked a caterer."

Tessa returned his smile, knowing he still hadn't recovered from the shock of receiving the caterer's bill. "We sure did, thanks to you. Let's go tell Katie."

Grabbing her hand, he tugged her toward the car. "Not

until I take you to dinner. Do you realize we've been so concerned about finding a caterer we forgot all about lunch?"

She muffled a snicker. "We did, didn't we? Are you sure you can afford it?"

He grinned. "I still have a little bit of pocket change. How about that Chinese restaurant we used to go to on Friday nights? You always liked their food."

She pulled back her sleeve and checked the time. "I'd like to, Mike, but I really need to pick up my car and go home and check the answering machine. The pastor was supposed to call me once he confirmed our use of the fellowship hall for the rehearsal dinner."

"No problem. I'll run you by the house, you can check the machine, and then I'll take you to dinner. We'll get your car later."

Tessa hesitated. The time the two had spent together, so far, had been because Katie had requested it. What he was proposing was different. Dare she accept his invitation and risk an informal evening with him? Though she'd never been able to forgive him, she still loved him. But he was still a cop—still working those long, demanding hours that drove her crazy. Nothing in their relationship had changed. If anything, it was worse due to their long estrangement. "I don't know, Mike. I'm sure you have things to do, and I really need to get back—"

"You have to eat, Tessie. Come on. Pig out on Chinese food with me. Umm, Crab Rangoon, doesn't that sound good? It's your favorite."

He remembered!

Mike gave her a tantalizing smile. "Sure beats eating leftovers alone."

❧

You want to come in?" Tessa asked when they pulled into her

driveway. "No sense waiting out here in the car."

Mike nodded and pushed his door open, surprised that she had invited him. He stepped inside the house and gave a quick glance around.

"Make yourself comfortable," she told him once they were inside. She moved to the answering machine and pressed the button. Katie's voice came on.

"Hi, Mom. It's me. How did the trip to the caterer go? Okay, I hope. Surely one of those caterers I listed came through for us."

Mike laughed at her comment. "Good thing she put several on the list!"

"Mom," Katie's voice continued, "I know this is hard for you, working with Daddy and being around him, but I want you to know I appreciate it."

The smile on his face faded.

"I hated it that Daddy wasn't around when I was little. My friends at church and the kids at school had daddies who were there for them. I didn't. I love you for always being there."

Katie snickered. "Especially the night you took me to the father-daughter banquet at church. Remember how we sat there, me wearing my brand-new red dress and patent leather shoes, waiting for Daddy, hoping he'd remember his promise to be there on time to pick me up? Then, when he didn't show, rather than have me disappointed, *you* took me. Looking back, I'm sure you were as embarrassed as I was when you were the only female father in the fellowship hall. But you graciously explained to anyone who asked that something came up and Daddy couldn't get away."

Mike looked in Tessa's direction, but she was standing with her back to him, her head in her hands. He could tell Katie's words had touched her, too.

"Oh, Mom, I couldn't bear it if he didn't show up for my

wedding. He's disappointed me so many times I couldn't begin to count them. I know his job is demanding and important, but I never understood why he quit going to church with us. I think that hurt more than anything."

Mike felt as if a dagger was being jabbed into his heart and twisted, and his life's blood was spilling onto the floor. He'd had no idea his absences in her life had affected her this deeply.

Tessa reached for the answering machine.

"No! Let it play!" Mike nearly shouted at her.

Misty eyes met his. "But, Mike—"

"Let it play," he repeated, this time keeping his voice down to a reasonable level.

She nodded, and again turned away from him.

"But, Mom—I'm gonna say this now because I don't know if I'd get through it in person without you stopping me— we can't continue being angry with Daddy for things that happened so long ago. God wants us to put those things aside and forgive him. No matter how hard that might be. And I want Daddy to be as much a part of my life as you are, Mom. Especially now that Jim and I are to be married. I want our family to come together. Of course, I want you and Daddy to be reconciled, but if that can't happen, at least I want you two to be civil to each other. We need to be able to be in the same room without hateful words and accusations ricocheting off the walls. I want us to celebrate Christmases, holidays, and birthdays together." Katie's falsetto laugh echoed through the tension-filled room. "I sound like one of those Miss America contestants. Maybe I should add that I want world peace!"

Neither Mike nor Tessa joined in their daughter's laughter.

"Well, I'm not sure how much your answering machine will record. Maybe my long-winded message was cut off several minutes ago, and you won't even hear this part. But—if you do, Mom—I want you to know I love and respect both of you. I know I've hurt you at times, and I apologize. I realize I hurt both you and Daddy, and especially God, by moving in with Jim before we were married—that's one reason I want to marry him as soon as possible. That and I wanted to be married on Christmas Day, like you and Daddy. Be kind to Daddy. I so want him to come back to the Lord, and I know you do, too. Call me when you get home."

As the machine clicked, signaling the end of Katie's message, Tessa rushed from the room, in tears, leaving Mike alone with his thoughts.

six

Mike felt numb, thoroughly chastised, and very much alone. And he felt bad for Tessa.

He pushed back in the recliner and stared through watery eyes at the room. The very recliner he sat in had been a gift from his wife. It was his chair. No one else was allowed to sit in it. On the table beside the chair was his Bible, also a gift from Tessa. She'd given it to him on their tenth anniversary. He'd loved that Bible. Flipping open its pages, he found numerous notations he'd made in the margins. Notations he'd made while listening to their pastor on Sunday mornings or doing his early morning scripture readings and meditations at home. He'd highlighted James 4:8 on the open page that lay in his hand: "Draw near to God and He will draw near to you."

Is that where I began to go wrong, Lord? When I quit communing with You and ceased reading Your Word? He carefully closed the Bible and placed it back on the table, making sure to put it in the exact same spot.

Next, his gaze went to the clock on the wall. The clock he had given Tessa the year they moved into their house. What a time he'd had hanging that clock. She'd wanted it mounted directly on the brick fireplace. When he'd told her it was impossible, she had put it in the hall closet where it had remained until one evening when Ellen and Bill had come for a visit. When she'd mentioned the clock to him and where she'd wanted it, Bill had asked her to bring him the drill and, within a few minutes, the clock was hanging on the fireplace in the very place she'd wanted it. Mike remembered how foolish he'd felt. He could have put that clock there himself but instead of admitting he didn't know how to mount it there, he'd lied and told her the job was impossible.

The matching sofas caught his attention. He could never imagine why anyone would want matching sofas. Two sofas in one room seemed foolish to him, but that's what Tessa had wanted. Though he'd bought them for her, he'd never admitted how wonderful that pair of sofas had been in their home. They made the perfect conversation area, the way they faced one another in front of the fireplace. Why hadn't he told her how much he'd grown to like them? Tessa had gone out of her way to make their house a home, doing the decorating herself, scouting out bargains at garage sales and flea markets. Every nook and cranny of their home was warm and inviting, and he'd barely been there to enjoy it.

He glanced at the wall over the desk and was surprised to see how many of his framed commendations were still hanging there. She hadn't taken them down! Why not?

Across the room on an upper shelf in the bookcase sat two glass bluebirds, mementos of their honeymoon. Though he'd been short on cash when they'd taken their honeymoon to Thousand Oaks, he'd managed to buy those bluebirds for Tessa, and she'd kept them all these years, displayed in one of the most prominent places in the room.

Other items about the room caught his eye. Most were filled with memories, symbols of the happier times of their marriage. Others were simply decorative pieces, but all were treasures of the past.

Pulling himself out of his reverie, he stood, embarrassed and ready to depart without saying good-bye, but he remembered Tessa's car, which was still parked in his apartment's lot. He couldn't leave. She'd be stranded without transportation. And what would Katie think of him if Tessa told her he hadn't taken her back to get her car?

"Tessie," he whispered softly toward the hall.

When she didn't respond, he whispered her name a little louder.

Still no response.

Not sure what to do, he tiptoed down the hall toward the bedroom he'd shared with his wife. A room he hadn't seen for eight long years. There was Tessa, stretched across the bed on her stomach, her face buried in the pillow shams, and she was sobbing like her heart was broken.

Mike stood in the doorway, his arms dangling by his sides. "Tessa," he repeated softly. "Are you—okay?"

"I–I'm fine," she said between sobs.

"I was thinking of going."

"Th–that's probably a good idea."

"We have to get your car."

Sitting up slowly, she rubbed at her eyes and lifted her chin high. "D–don't worry about it. I'll get Ellen to ta–take me to pick it up."

He cautiously took a few steps toward her. "I'm sorry, Tessie. I know Katie's message upset you. It upset me, too. Please don't tell her I heard it."

"I—I don't want to discuss it, Mike. Please le–leave. I'll take care of getting my car."

He moved toward the bed. "Can I get you anything? A glass of water? An aspirin?"

"No, th–thank you. Go on home. We have a bu–busy day ahead of us tomorrow."

"You still want me to go to the—" His cell phone rang and, though he hated to answer it, he knew he had to. "Garrett."

He listened a moment, told the caller he'd be right there, and hung up.

"Duty calls?" Tessa asked, sniffing and lifting her tearstained face once more.

"Yeah, they wouldn't have called unless it was important. We've got another victim. They think it's the woman I've been looking for—the one who abandoned her physically abused four-month-old baby in a cardboard box at the bus station."

Tessa waved toward the door in a shooing motion. "Go on, Mike. Do what you have to do."

"I don't want to leave you this way."

She rubbed a hand across her tearstained face. "You were already leaving, Mike, before you got that call. Go."

"I'll have them get someone else to—" His phone rang again. "Garrett," he snapped impatiently. "Okay. Okay. Yes." He listened then shook his head sadly. "That's good. It should help us find her boyfriend. Thanks for letting me know. See you in a sec." He turned to Tessa, his face somber. "They found a picture in her pocket. Her, some guy, and the baby. I gotta go. If we don't hurry, the guy may get out of state. I'll call you in the morning about going to the florist." He hurried toward the door, turning only long enough to say again, "I'm really sorry."

"Yeah, me, too," he heard Tessa say as he headed down the hall toward the door.

"I would never have called you, Mike," the officer on duty told him as Mike bent over the Jane Doe, "especially since you're taking a few days off and asked that we not call, but I knew you'd be interested in this. Makes you wonder what would possess a woman to make her let a man do this to her. I'll bet that baby in this picture is the one we found at the bus station." He held the picture out toward Mike.

"Sure looks like the same baby." Mike examined the picture carefully then checked Jane Doe's face. Though she'd been badly beaten and her face was swollen and marred with dried blood, he was sure she was the woman in the picture.

"Somebody really had it in for this woman," the coroner said, standing and pulling off his latex gloves. "I hope you get whoever did this."

"Notice anything that might help me get him?"

The man nodded. "He was wearing a big ring."

Mike rubbed at his chin thoughtfully. "Anything else?"

"Don't know where it came from, maybe from the guy, but someone had spit a wad of chewing tobacco on her chest."

"Maybe the lab tech can tell us what brand. That might help. Might even find a DNA match."

The coroner tossed his gloves into a bag and sealed it. "I'll bag the sample and get it to him right away."

Mike knelt and stared at the woman. "We humans do horrible things to one another, don't we?"

The duty officer huffed. "Tell me about it. I've seen more strange and cruel behavior in the five years I've been on the force than I expected I'd see in a lifetime. Wives stabbing husbands. Husbands strangling wives. Makes you wonder how these people ever got together in the first place. Don't couples usually get married because they love each other and want to be together? Kids are even killing their parents. What's this world coming to?"

"Good question."

"Well, every time one of these tragedies happens, I go home and thank the Lord for my wife and kids and our happy home. I'm way more blessed than any man deserves to be."

"You are a lucky man. I hope you know that." Mike gave the pitiful victim one final glance then rose. "I'm heading to the station. I'll probably be there most of the night. Call me if anything else comes up."

On the way across town he drove past Tessa's house, still guilt-ridden for leaving her stranded without transportation. But there it was, her car, parked in her driveway. Maybe she'd called Ellen for a ride just as she said. All he knew was he'd let her down—again.

As promised, Mike phoned Tessa the next morning, fearful she might not answer when she noticed his number on her caller ID.

"You really don't have to go to the florist with me," she told him coolly. "I'm sure, what with the important case you're working on, you have things to do that can't wait."

"No, Tessie, I want to go with you. If anything further develops, the guys will call me."

After a bit of hesitation, she agreed to let him pick her up and drive her to the florist rather than take her own car.

Merry Sinclair, the owner of Forget-Me-Not Florist Shop and a member of their church, greeted them warmly as they came through the door.

"It's good to see you both," Merry said as the two women greeted one another with a hug. "I was really happy when Katie phoned and said she and Jim had decided to get married," the woman told her with an understanding smile. "But you certainly have your work cut out for you, putting together a formal Christmas Day wedding in such a short time."

"Then you'll be able to help us?"

"Of course, I'll help you. What are friends for? Besides, my son and his wife aren't going to be able to come for Christmas until the twenty-sixth so I was going to spend Christmas Day by myself. Helping with Katie and Jim's wedding will be a lot more fun." She motioned toward a large refrigerated case along the far wall. "Katie mentioned red roses and white carnations. She was so adamant about it I figured there must be some special symbolism involved."

Mike had to smile when Tessa ducked her head shyly. "We—Mike and I—had red roses and white carnations at our wedding."

"On Christmas Day," he added.

Merry sent him a smile. "Red roses and white carnations make a lovely setting for a Christmas wedding. I think Katie has made a wonderful choice. For major impact and to take advantage of the traditional red and green Christmas colors, for the sanctuary I would suggest a gigantic arrangement on each side of the altar, tall red candles in the candelabra with fresh green ivy intertwined, and red roses, white carnations, and more ivy anchored with huge red bows at the end of each pew."

Tessa nodded and from the look on her face Mike could see she agreed with each suggestion Merry was making. "Would you use the same colors and flowers for the wedding party's corsages and boutonnieres?"

"Definitely." Merry pulled a single long-stemmed red rose from the case and handed it to Tessa. "And I'll get together with Jim and make sure he uses the same combination for a lovely, vine-trailing bridal bouquet for Katie. How does that sound?"

"Expensive!" Mike rubbed at his chin. "Do we have to use so many flowers?"

Tessa gave him a look. *That* look.

He shrugged. "Sorry, Merry, but it seems this whole thing is mushrooming out of control. I don't want to look like a skinflint, but I'm not Mr. Moneybags. Cops don't make as much money as most folks think we do."

He was surprised when Merry gave him a pleasant smile instead of looking at him like he had two heads.

"I completely understand, Mike. So many times I see folks spend way more than they should on a wedding for their children. I hate to see people go into debt." She placed her hand on his shoulder placatingly. "Don't you worry about it. We'll use silk flowers and ivy wherever we can. I doubt anyone will even notice. I'll go get a few pieces from the stockroom so you can see what I have in mind."

From the look on Tessa's face, Mike knew he was in for it once Merry was out of earshot.

"Do you have to sing your poor song to everyone we meet?"

Her words stung. "I'm not claiming poverty, Tessie. At least, I don't mean to. I'm just being truthful."

Her expression softened a bit. "Look, Mike. I know this wedding is going to cost way more than you expected, and I can understand your concern. But this constant complaining about the costs embarrasses me, and I'd think would embarrass you. I'm not used to discussing our finances with anyone, especially friends from church."

He took a step toward her, nearly knocking a huge Oriental vase filled with colorful silk flowers off a nearby display table, catching hold of it just in time. "Look, Tessie. I'm sorry. I mean it. The last thing I want to do is embarrass you *or* Katie."

"Here they are." Merry hurried toward them, a lovely bouquet cradled in her arms. "Aren't these pretty?"

Tessa reached out, gently touching several of the blossoms' petals. "They *are* silk! I would never have guessed it. They're beautiful."

"Yeah, those sure look real," Mike chimed in approvingly.

"Many brides actually prefer silk flowers to fresh ones. In addition to a savings in cost, with a little care the flowers literally last forever. Some brides have us rearrange all the flowers into bouquets after the wedding and use them as floral arrangements about their home. They make wonderful mementos of one of the happiest days of their lives."

Mike took a single red rose from Merry's hand and examined it carefully. "Tessie, you think Katie would go for these?"

"I think so. I couldn't say for sure."

"I'll box up a few of these so you can show them to Katie."

Mike grinned. "Good idea."

"They are beautiful, and they do look real," Tessa told him as Merry scurried off toward the back room again. "But there's no fragrance. Nothing can duplicate the exquisite aroma of the real thing."

"Yeah, you're right."

"Well, let's not worry about it now. We'll let Katie make that decision."

"Tessie?"

"Yes?"

"Don't mention my complaining or the difference in cost when we show these to Katie, okay?"

She frowned. "But I thought that was the reason we were considering silk."

"It was, but I want Katie to have whichever kind she chooses."

She tilted her head quizzically. "You're sure about that?"

"Absolutely."

"Then I won't mention it."

He gave her a grateful smile. "Thanks, Tessie."

She returned his smile. "You're welcome."

He sent her a sideways grin. "You know what?"

"What?"

"Seeing Merry holding those flowers in her arms like that reminded me of you on our wedding day. You sure were beautiful."

Her eyes widened. "Uh—thank you, Mike."

The shy smile and look on her face sent chills down his spine. As much as he hated to admit it, he still loved that woman.

"Here you are." Merry handed a long white box to Mike. "Tell Katie to call me if she has any questions. I hope she knows how lucky she is to have the two of you helping her. Where are you off to now?"

"The photographer," they answered in unison.

❧

Tessa glanced at Mike as they sat waiting in the lobby of the Creative Images Photo Shop. "I've heard great things about this photographer. He photographed Valene and Jordan's wedding as well as Vanessa and Nathan's. He did Della and Brandon's wedding, too. Ellen said he was great to work with and highly recommended him."

"I still don't understand why Katie has to use a professional photographer. Jim said Bill Zobel has a brand-new digital camera. Why doesn't Katie let him take pictures? I've heard those new digital cameras do a great job. Didn't Nathan take video of Jordan and Valene's wedding? Maybe he'd shoot video of Katie and Jim's."

Tessa stared at him in the same quizzical way she'd stared at him at the caterer. "You've got to be kidding! For truly professional wedding photographs, you have to have top-quality cameras, special lighting, knowledge of settings and how to group people—all sorts of things."

"Hello." A handsome young man in a black turtleneck pullover and black trousers greeted them with a smile. "I'm Eric. What can I do for you?"

"We need you to photograph our daughter's wedding," Mike said after a quick glance in his wife's direction. "Several of her friends recommended you."

"And when is this wedding to be?"

"Christmas Day."

"Well, we are planning things early, aren't we? A full year in advance? Most people only give us a few months' notice. Unfortunately, we never shoot a wedding on Christmas Day!"

"It's this Christmas Day," Tessa said quickly.

His mouth gaping, the man stared at them. "That's not even two weeks off!"

"Isn't there some way you could do it?" Mike asked, almost wishing the man would say no so he could ask Bill to do it with his digital camera.

"On Christmas Day? No! My mother and father would never forgive me if I didn't show up at their house on Christmas Day!"

Tessa looked as if she were about to cry. "Can you recommend another photographer who would be willing to do it on Christmas Day?"

The man thought for a moment. "Not a one. Sorry."

"Now what?" Tessa asked once they were both back in the car. "And don't say anything about having Bill and Nathan do it. They can take all the extra pictures you want them to, but we must have a professional photographer for Katie's wedding. She loved the other couples' pictures. That girl has her heart set on this Eric fellow doing it. What if we can't find another photographer? What then?"

Mike watched as Tessa blinked a few times; then he turned and climbed out of the car. "I'll be right back."

He entered the shop and found the man still standing at the counter. "Look, Eric, Katie is my only daughter. She's laid up at home with a broken ankle and has had to depend on her mother and me to do the footwork for this wedding. She's seen the work you've done for her friends and she wants you to be her photographer."

"Most brides begin planning their wedding months ahead of time. Why did she wait so long? Two weeks is not much notice at any time of year, but especially in December." Eric gave Mike a look of disgust, but he ignored it. He didn't want to alienate the man when he was about to try to bargain with him.

"Long story, which I won't go into now, but take it from me, Katie and Jim *are* going to be married on Christmas Day." Mike pulled his credit card from his wallet and held it out toward the man. "What's it going to take to get you to be the one to photograph it?"

Five minutes later, he climbed back into the car. "The guy's gonna do it after all."

"He is? On Christmas Day? How did you get him to change his mind?"

Momentarily putting aside the thought of the exorbitant amount of money he'd had to promise the man to get him to cancel his plans to be with his parents on Christmas Day in order to be Katie's official photographer, he gave her a victorious smile. "Just had a little man-to-man talk with him. That's all."

Tessa scooted toward him, her face beaming with delight. "Mike, I don't know how you talked him into it but thank you. Katie will be so pleased." Bracing herself on the console between them, she pushed herself up and kissed him on the cheek. "I'm pleased, too. More than I can tell you."

For the first time in more than eight years, Mike felt like a king. Whatever this wedding was going to cost him, it would be worth it, just to be back in Tessa's good graces, if even for a moment. "Good. What's next on our agenda?"

"Actually, we're pretty well finished. All of the really important things have been taken care of. We still have to select and purchase the various gifts for the wedding party, but we can do that tomorrow. The most important thing left to do is address the rest of the wedding invitations. Katie has already mailed hers to their friends and associates, but she's asked us to do the rest. We need to get them in the mail by tomorrow at the latest. Even then, we'll be giving people extremely short notice."

"She isn't going over the two hundred and fifty mark we told the caterer, is she?"

Tessa laughed and slapped at his arm playfully. "No! I think she said her list consisted of about two hundred names. That means you and I will have to keep our list down to about fifty."

"That shouldn't be too hard," Mike said with confidence.

In no time they reached Tessa's house.

"Look, Mike," Tessa said, giving him a warm smile as he pulled the car into her driveway, "you've amazed me by the way you've put your detective work on hold this week. I know you have things that need to be done, and I have a few things to tend to, as well. Let's take the rest of the day off."

"What about the invitations?"

"I was about to suggest you come to the house for supper tonight. We could work on them then."

Her invitation was welcome—and something he certainly hadn't expected. "Yeah, that'd be nice," he said, savoring her words. "What time?"

"Six okay?"

"I'll be there!"

❧

Tessa felt as nervous as a contestant in a cooking contest as she did one more final check through the house, making sure everything was in place. Why she invited Mike to dinner, she'd never understand. But she had, and now she'd have to go through with it.

When the doorbell rang at exactly six, she took a quick glance in the hall mirror, smoothed at her hair with her fingertips, and then hurried to open the door.

"Hi." Mike stepped inside, a small bouquet of fresh red roses gripped tightly in his hands. "Got them at the gas station. They didn't have white carnations."

Her heart racing, she took them and lifted them to sniff their sweet fragrance. "Thank you, Mike. I love them."

"You're welcome." His smile turned to a frown. "I've been thinking. Maybe the silk flowers aren't such a good idea for Katie's wedding. I sure like the smell of the real ones."

"But think of the difference in price," she reminded him, clutching the flowers to her breast, still amazed that he would do something so thoughtful. "Silk won't be so bad."

He moved closer to her and sniffed the air. "Is that meat loaf I smell?"

"Sure is."

"I haven't had your meat loaf—"

"For over eight years," Tessa interrupted, finishing his sentence and putting a little distance between the two of them. "Since Katie moved out, I rarely fix it for myself. It'll be nice to have someone to share it with." She uttered a nervous laugh. "But don't expect lemon meringue pie. I didn't have time to bake one."

"Hey, I really don't care what we're having. Just you inviting me here is enough. I've—I've missed being in our home."

She noticed he nearly choked when she ducked her head and in a voice nearly inaudible said, "I've missed having you here." Had those words really come from her mouth? Gathering her wits about her, she pushed past him toward the kitchen. "Make yourself comfortable. I'll have things on the table in a minute."

Tessa leaned against the refrigerator and tried to catch her breath. She couldn't let herself be drawn into Mike's erratic lifestyle again, no matter how much she wanted to be there. It didn't work then—it wouldn't work now. Nothing had changed, except she had grown older, lonelier, and more vulnerable. No matter how much she claimed otherwise, she didn't like being alone.

"Want some help?" Mike appeared in the doorway a few minutes later, looking every bit as handsome—except for the paunch he'd acquired over the years—as he had eight years ago.

"You're just in time. Dinner is ready."

They laughed their way through their meal, reminiscing about the early years of their marriage, Katie's birth, and the good times they'd had together, each clearly going out of their way to avoid any mention of the bad times.

"I'm stuffed," Mike finally said, pushing back in his chair and rubbing his belly. "That meat loaf was fantastic! Everything was. My compliments to the cook."

Tessa felt herself blushing as she mouthed a demure, "Thank you."

Mike helped her with the dishes, something he'd never even considered doing before, as she recalled; then the two of them moved into the family room to get started on the invitations.

"Who would you like to invite, Mike?" Tessa picked up the pad she'd left on the coffee table and poised her pen over it.

He screwed up his face thoughtfully. "I dunno. Captain Ferrell and his wife, I guess. Four or five other detectives and their wives. That's about it. Oh, and the police chief and his wife. I nearly forgot him!"

Tessa wrote down all the names and information while Mike looked up the addresses in the phone book. "Now that you've completed your list, we can start on mine." She pulled her address book from the table, flipping through the pages slowly. "Our assistant pastor and his family. Ellen and Bill Zobel. Katie probably already added them to her list. Our neighbors on both sides. . . The Reeds across the street. . ."

She went on to add a second entire page to her list, most of them friends from church she knew weren't on Katie's or Jim's lists, while Mike looked on.

Finally, with a cautioning smile, he gave her a tap on the shoulder. "You do realize your list alone has way over fifty people on it?"

She scanned the names. "Oh, Mike, I'm sorry. I hadn't realized."

"I hate this, Tessa. Even if I could afford adding more names, I'm not sure the caterer would agree to serve more than two hundred and fifty on Christmas Day."

She started at the top of her list, crossing off a name here and there. "I'm sure I can eliminate a few names, but I don't want to offend anyone by not inviting them. And there are so many others I'd like to invite that I haven't even added to this list."

He let out a sigh. "Me, too. I've thought of at least ten others since I finished my list. Keeping this wedding down to a reasonable size is hopeless."

"I still have that piece of property up near Turner Falls my aunt left me. Maybe I could sell it and—"

"No, absolutely not," Mike answered firmly, his hand grasping her wrist tightly. "I know how much that piece of land means to you. Don't worry about it, Tessie. I'll come up with the money."

"But I—"

He pressed his finger to her lips. "Not another word. I'll call the caterer tomorrow and ask if we can add another twenty five to our total."

"But Katie doesn't—"

"Not a word about this to Katie, understood?"

She gave him a nod. How nice it was to have Mike taking charge and being an active part of her life again. If only he'd done this years ago.

"I'll pick you up about nine tomorrow," he told her when they'd finished their lists.

"You really don't need to go with me, Mike. All I'm going to do is shop for gift items for the members of Katie's wedding party, the candles for the candelabra, the guest book for the reception, and a myriad of other last-minute things on Katie's list. I know how much you hate shopping. Let me take care of those things."

He shook his head. "No, I want to help. I wonder how Katie is getting along with her walking cast."

"She's doing fine. I talked to her first thing this morning. She says it's much better than having to hold her foot up and hobble around with the walker. Too bad it was her right foot so she can't drive, at least she's able to get around the condo more easily. That really helps. She wanted to go shopping with me, but I encouraged her to stay home and concentrate on any final wedding details."

"Good idea. Are you sure you don't need any help? I'm still willing."

"No, I'll manage just fine. Oh, by the way, Katie and Jim want us to have dinner with them tomorrow night. She said Jim is cooking. Can you make it?"

"Dinner with you two nights in a row? Sure I can make it. What time?"

"About seven."

"Want me to come by for you?"

She shook her head. "No thanks. I want to stop by Ellen's

on the way and return a book I borrowed. I'll meet you at Katie's."

❧

Tessa greeted Mike at Katie's door when he arrived the next evening, looking bright and fresh and prettier than he'd seen her in a long time. "Wow, you look terrific!" was all he could think to say. She took his breath away.

"Hi, Daddy."

Katie thumped her way to the door then gave his cheek a kiss, ending it with a childlike smacking sound that made him laugh. He might not have been the best father when she was growing up, but he loved his precious Katie dearly and wanted to make things up to her. "Hi, pumpkin. Sure nice to see you up and around. How's the ankle?"

"Doin' good." Katie gave him a generous smile. "I'll be able to walk down the aisle with no trouble at all." She motioned toward the little dining area where the table was beautifully set with glowing candles and colorful place mats. "Jim's out on the patio turning the steaks. Dinner should be ready in no time. Would you like some iced tea or a cup of coffee?"

"Iced tea would be. . ." He stopped to answer his cell phone. "Garrett."

Mike listened a minute, excited to hear the news the chief of detectives was giving him on the other end, then said good-bye and hung up, disappointed he wouldn't be able to have dinner with his family after all. "Gotta go," he told Katie and Tessa as he headed for the door. "That was my boss. We finally got a big break in the case I've been working on. They need me at the station to interrogate a new witness. I'm really sorry. I'll try—"

Tessa's face grew red as her hands anchored on her hips. "Mike, you're doing it again! Jim and Katie have worked hard to prepare this dinner for us and you're leaving?"

"Mom!"

Mike shot her a troubled frown. "You think I want to leave? With you and Katie and Jim here and those fabulous steaks cooking on the grill?"

Tessa jutted out her chin. "But you *are* leaving, aren't you?"

"Daddy has to go, Mom! Why do you always make a big deal out it? It's his job!"

"Because it always was a big deal, Katie. Did you ever tell him how many times you cried yourself to sleep because he ran off to some crime scene when you needed him? When you had a ball game or a school play, or something else important to you?"

Katie blushed and glanced toward her father but remained silent.

"I was there," Tessa went on. "I knew what you were going through. I was going through it, too! We could never count on your father to be there when we needed him. His work was more important than we were. We always took second place."

Obviously upset at being placed in the middle, Katie glared at her mother. "That's not fair."

Trying to keep from saying words he'd regret later, Mike crossed the room and stopped in the doorway. "I'm sorry, Katie. I never meant for this to happen," he told her in a level tone, "but this case affects a lot of people in our community. I can't go into detail, but believe me, it's important, or I wouldn't be interrogating this witness myself. I'll call you later."

Just before closing the door, he glanced in Tessa's direction. "I'll call you in the morning."

❧

Infuriated by his sudden departure, Tessa clenched and unclenched her fists at her sides as she stared at the closed door. To her, it was as if history was repeating itself all over again, and she didn't like it one bit better now than she had years ago.

"I'd hoped, when I arranged for you and Daddy to spend time together, the two of you would begin to get along, but I can see I was wrong. It was a waste of effort," Katie told her, leaning against the table as she lowered herself into a chair. "You're both as stubborn as you ever were."

Tessa turned to gape at her daughter. "What do you mean—arranged for your father and me to spend time together?"

"Mom, surely you didn't think I was as helpless as I appeared! Yes, I broke my ankle, but did it ever occur to you that I could have phoned the caterer and the florist and the photographer? Vanessa and Valene begged me to let them help, but I saw this whole thing as an opportunity to bring the two of you together! The two people I love most in the whole world, next to Jim, of course."

Tessa felt her heartbeat quicken as she stared openmouthed at her daughter. "You tricked us? Katie, how could you? You knew how I felt about your father!"

Katie met her intense stare with one of her own. "I should know how you felt. You've told me often enough." The expression on her face softened as she reached out and took her mother's hand in hers. "Mom, it's time to move on. From the time I was a little girl, you've tried to convince me God was in control of your life, but He hasn't been. He was only in control as long as He allowed you to call the shots."

Shocked and hurt, Tessa found it hard to speak but finally the words, though difficult, came out. "I can't believe you would say such a thing. I love the Lord with my whole heart. Surely you remember all the times I worked at the church, doing many jobs others refused to do, all the years I've taught Sunday school, the dinners I've cooked and taken to the sick, the many people from our congregation I've visited at the hospital."

"Granted, Mom, those are all wonderful things, but were all

those things done for God? Or did you do them because you enjoyed them and they filled a void in your life?"

Tessa squared her shoulders and lifted her chin. "I did them for God, Katie! I can't imagine why you'd ask me such a thing! I'm a Christian!"

Katie turned loose of her mother's hand and leaned back in her chair. "I'm not saying these things to hurt you. Honest, I'm not. But, Mom, I accepted the Lord as my Savior when I was a child, and I meant it. I actually asked Him to forgive my sins and come into my heart, but with all the fighting and bickering going on in our home when I was a little girl, I began to wonder if God were real. If He was, why would my parents, who I thought loved each other and who both claimed to be Christians, behave in such an ugly way toward each other? I felt like we were playing church, like actors in a play—that what our family had was not the real thing at all, but the actions and speech expected of us because everyone thought we were good people, and good people were supposed to attend church."

Tessa searched her heart and came up short. Had she really done all those things, those works, simply to glorify and draw attention to herself? To solicit the praises of other people instead of performing them to please God? What had she done to her daughter? Were her actions and those of Mike, responsible for Katie pulling away from the God she had assumed her daughter loved? "Is—is that the reason you quit going to church? Because I let you down?"

Katie hung her head, avoiding her mother's eyes. "That was one of the reasons. I was disillusioned with the church, you, Daddy, my so-called Christian friends, all of it. But mainly it was because of some of the things I got into in high school—things I've never told you about. Things I knew displeased God."

Tessa's jaw dropped. "Katie Garrett! Whatever do you mean? I had no idea you'd ever been in trouble!"

"Only because I never told you! I was great at hiding things from you, and Daddy was never home, so I didn't have to worry about him finding out."

Unable to even comprehend that her sweet, innocent teen-aged daughter could have been guilty of any wrongdoing, Tessa simply stared at her. "You must tell me, Katie. I have to know. What did you do when you were a teenager?"

seven

A number of things I'm not very proud of, but I guess the worst was during the Christmas break of my junior year."

Tessa's heart sank. "Oh, Katie—from the look on your face, I'm almost afraid to hear it."

"You remember when you thought I went skiing with the Clarkson family to Colorado? Well, I—"

"You *did* go to Colorado with them, didn't you? Oh, please say you did."

Katie fiddled with a fingernail and seemed to be avoiding Tessa's eyes. "Not exactly."

Her patience wearing thin, Tessa reached out and cupped her daughter's chin with her hand, lifting her face. "What do you mean—not exactly? Either you did or you didn't."

"I had planned to go with them," Katie confessed, still avoiding her mother's eyes, "but at the last minute, Mr. Clarkson had to cancel. He ended up having gallbladder surgery. Since his wife wanted to stay with him, he let us take his van, and we three girls went on alone."

Tessa gasped. "Without a chaperone? Clear to Colorado? Oh, Katie, if I'd known I would never have let you go!"

Katie hung her head, a guilt-ridden look on her face. "That's the reason I didn't tell you. But there's more."

Tessa sucked in a deep breath. "What else, Katie? I need to hear all of it."

"We—we met some really cute twenty-year-old guys and

drove all around the mountains with them in their SUV. I know it was dumb but—"

"Katie! You were sixteen! Please tell me nothing happened."

"Sorry, Mom, but it did. I tasted alcohol for the first time and after a few drinks, I found I liked it."

Tessa's mind reeled. "I don't like the direction this is going, Katie Garrett."

"I've wanted to get this off my chest for a long time. I hate to admit it, Mom, but I got drunk as a skunk. It was a dumb thing to do but, at the time, it really seemed cool. And yes, I know all the things that could have happened to me, but they didn't. I guess your prayers were protecting me. Even now, I shudder to think what might have happened." The guilty look on Katie's face twisted into a slight smile. "Actually, all three of us girls got so sick we vomited all over that new SUV. Those guys literally dumped us off at the hotel, and we never saw them again."

Aghast at her daughter's confession, Tessa imagined all kinds of scenarios, sending her mind spinning. "Is that the whole truth, Katie? You're not covering something up, are you?"

"Just one other tiny thing."

Tessa's hand went to her forehead. "Oh, no. What?"

"Those stupid jocks drove off with our purses. We didn't have money to pay the hotel bill or purchase gas for the drive home. So—"

Still in awe of what she was hearing, Tessa gave her head an accusing shake. "I guess I'd have to say you deserved it, taking up with strangers like that. So you called the Clarksons?"

Katie lifted wide eyes to meet hers. "No, I called Dad."

"You called your father? Why, Katie? You could have called me!"

Katie gave her head a vigorous shake. "No way, Mom. You

would have had a coronary! It was bad enough having to call Dad. Believe me! Though he wired me the money, he read me the riot act. Big-time!"

"You turned to your father instead of me?" Tessa asked, both angered and hurt that Katie had contacted Mike. "Why, Katie? Why would you do such a thing? Haven't I always been the one who was there for you?"

After propping her foot up on the ottoman, Katie leaned her head against the back of the sofa and didn't answer for a moment. "Mom," she said finally, "yes, you've always been there for me, and I love you for it, but why can't you understand I love Daddy, too? He may not have been there the many times I wished he would have been, but he's worked hard all his life to provide the kind of lifestyle he's wanted for me. Because of Dad's willingness to provide for our needs, you were able to be a stay-at-home mom and never had to work like most of my friends' moms did."

Tessa swallowed hard. Every word Katie was saying was true.

"If he'd been an accountant, a lawyer, or even a plumber like you and Grandpa wanted him to be, maybe he would have worked regular hours. But he didn't, Mom, and he would have hated it. From the time Daddy was a little boy he wanted to be a policeman. You told me yourself, you knew that long before you two were engaged. Did you expect him to forget his dream just because the two of you got married? I sure hope Jim never does that to me!"

"I—I hoped he'd forget about it once we were married. Especially after you were born," Tessa shot back defensively.

"Mom! That was an unrealistic expectation! What if Dad had decided he wanted *you* to become a waitress? Or maybe a flight attendant? Would you have accepted that?" Crossing her arms over her chest, Katie huffed. "I think not! Not you! You're much too independent. Thanks to Daddy, you've always done pretty much as you pleased."

Though the words stung, Tessa had no counterargument. For the most part, she had done whatever she'd wished all her life, with neither her parents nor Mike stepping in to even try to change her mind.

"Perhaps it'd be wise if we let this subject drop. I doubt you and I will ever see eye-to-eye when it comes to Daddy." Katie grabbed onto the arm of the sofa and struggled to her feet. "Make yourself comfortable, Mom. I'm going to check on the steaks."

Tessa's eyes filled with tears as she watched her lovely daughter hobble across the room and out the patio door. What had started out as a lovely evening had turned into a nightmare because she had lost control and exploded at Mike over that phone call. Why hadn't she kept her mouth shut? *We've been separated for over eight years. I have absolutely no right to question what he does and why, any more than he should tell me what to do.*

Slowly she crossed the room and gazed at the framed picture her daughter had placed prominently on the fireplace mantel— a picture of the three of them on Katie's tenth birthday. What a wonderful day that had been. They'd had so much fun celebrating. How handsome Mike had looked in his blue plaid shirt. As usual, his hair was badly in need of a cut. She smiled at the funny little way his mouth always turned up when he posed for a photograph. He hated having his picture taken.

Lifting the frame from the mantel, she pressed it to her heart. With a tear rolling down her cheek, she closed her eyes and whispered, "I'll always love you, Mike Garrett. Though I've tried to fight it and not admit it to myself, being with you these past few days has only made me realize how much

I still love you. No one will ever be able to take your place in my heart."

ও

Tessa leaped to answer the phone when it rang at seven the next morning. It was Mike.

"Hi. I hope I'm not calling too early. I was at the station all night, and I'm bushed. I really need a couple hours of shut-eye. I heard you say you still had a few things to purchase. I— I wonder if it'd be okay if we put off the rest of our shopping for those last things on Katie's list until this afternoon?"

Remembering she had abandoned all rights to Mike's time when they'd separated, she answered quietly, "That would be fine or, like I said, I can finish myself. There's not that much to do."

"No." His answer was firm. "Katie asked me to help you, and that's what I intend to do. I'll be there by one o'clock." The phone clicked in her ear.

As promised, Mike appeared at her door at one, looking rested and ready to go, a pleasant smile on his face. "Look, I'm sorry about last night. Not that it's any excuse but this case I'm working on has made me crazy. I had no right to snap at you that way."

Her heart doing a leap, she returned his smile as she led him into the room and seated herself beside him on the sofa. "I'm the one who should apologize. I had no right to criticize your actions."

To her surprise, Mike bent and placed a quick kiss on her forehead. "Let's pretend it never happened."

Though Tessa tried to hold it back, a broad smile broke forth. "I'd like that."

"What's on the agenda for today?"

"I finished most of the shopping yesterday, but we need

to pick up the rolls of white satin ribbon for decorating the church, and I need to purchase a pair of ivory shoes, and—"

Mike reared back with a laugh. "Guess we'd better hurry if we're gonna get all that stuff done." Still smiling, he extended an open palm.

A wave of pleasure swept over her as she placed her hand in his and they headed for the door.

❧

Tessa awoke early the next morning after enjoying one of the best night's sleep she'd had in a long time. She actually let out a giggle as she remembered the good time she'd had with Mike as they'd gone from one store to another, crossing off the things on both hers and their daughter's list. Not one time had Mike's cell phone rung, which she was grateful for. She wondered if he'd threatened those at his office to only call in case of a dire emergency.

Though Mike hadn't mentioned he would call her, she leaped to answer the phone when it rang at nine o'clock, half expecting it to be him.

"Mom! It's happened again!" It was obvious by the screech in Katie's voice something was radically wrong. "Della's shop just delivered the wrong gown!"

"Are you sure?" she asked, nearly as panic-stricken as her daughter.

"Of course I'm sure! This one has stupid-looking ruffles from head to toe and is made of some weird fabric."

"Now, honey, let's not overreact. I'm sure it's nothing more than a simple mistake. Have you called Della?"

Katie sniffled. "I've tried a dozen times, but the line is busy. What am I going to do, Mom? It seems everything is going wrong, and here I am with this stupid cast on my leg! I can't even drive."

"Don't worry, sweetie. I'll hop in the car and hurry over to Della's shop. I'm sure they just delivered your dress to another customer by mistake, and you'll have the right one in no time."

"You don't mind?"

"Not one bit. I'll call you from the shop."

In less than five minutes Tessa was in her car, inserting the key in the ignition.

But nothing happened.

No engine noise.

Nothing.

Now what? She lowered her head onto the steering wheel and closed her eyes. *Lord, please. I know You're displeased with me, but don't let this wedding fall apart.*

She turned the key again.

Still nothing.

She pulled out her cell phone and dialed Mike's number. He answered on the first ring.

After explaining about Katie's dress and the trouble with her car, she asked, "Can you come after me? I need to get over to the bridal shop as soon as possible. Katie is a basket case over this."

"I really want to, Tessie, but I can't," he explained, sounding genuinely sorry. "That guy I was interrogating just gave me some vital information that may solve the case. I have to check it out immediately. It could be the break I've been looking for."

She felt the old resentment rising. "Can't someone else do it?"

After a slight pause, Mike told her apologetically, "I'm afraid not. This is my case, and I don't want any slipups. I want to be there to personally make sure all the t's are crossed and the i's are dotted. When I get the guy I'm looking for, I don't want some fancy high-paid lawyer getting him off on a technicality. This guy deserves to be locked up for the rest of his life, and I'm going to make sure that happens."

Tessa clutched the phone tightly. "I'd think, just once in your life, you could put your family first, but I guess that's never going to happen. Forget it. I'll call a cab!" With that, she cut off their connection.

An hour later she arrived at Katie's condo, carrying the proper dress. "The delivery boy just delivered the two gowns to the wrong addresses. All it took was one quick phone call from Della, and the mystery was solved. She's sending him by later this afternoon to pick up the one he left for you."

Katie dabbed at her eyes with a tissue. "Thanks, Mom. I didn't mean to sound like such a baby on the phone, but so many things have gone wrong. I'd just had my fill."

Tessa sat down and slipped her arm about Katie's shoulders, giving her a much-needed hug. "It's okay, baby. Your dress is here, most of the things for your wedding are done, and you're marrying one of the nicest, most responsible men I've ever met. On your first wedding anniversary you and Jim will laugh at all the trouble you've had."

Katie wiped away another tear. "Dad called."

Tessa gave a flip of her hand. "So? What did the busy man have to say?"

"He was concerned about you. He told me about your car trouble."

"Did he tell you he refused to come and take me to Della's shop? That he was too busy playing detective?"

Katie let out a long sigh. "He's not *playing* detective, Mom. I don't know why you keep saying that. Daddy's work is important."

"More important than his family? Surely he's not the only competent detective on the police force. This is not about how important his job is. I think this is more about your father feeling important by playing his role as a detective. And it's the only role in life he's chosen to play. He's abandoned that of husband and father."

"I hate to say this, Mom. I don't mean to upset you, but I don't understand how you can call yourself a Christian and talk about Daddy the way you do. What about all the forgiveness God speaks about in the Bible? Doesn't He say we should forgive our enemies? And Daddy wasn't your enemy; he was your husband. Does all that scripture about forgiveness pertain to everyone but you?"

Tessa's hackles rose defensively. "Don't be insolent, Katie. You can't begin to know how badly your father hurt me."

"But, Mom! You still need to forgive him. He didn't do it intentionally. He loves you, and I know you still love him, and—"

"Where did you get that idea?"

Katie's lips twisted into a slight smile. "It's obvious, Mom. I can tell."

Tessa lifted her chin defiantly. "You're speaking foolishness, Katie Garrett."

"Yeah, sure."

"If your father had any love for me, he would have quit that job of his."

"And if you'd had any love for him, you would have put up with his crazy hours!" Katie shot back.

Tessa crossed her arms over her chest and turned her head away. Though she couldn't see Katie's face, she knew Katie was about to add more to her outrageous comment.

"You—and Daddy—are incorrigible. And stubborn. And afraid to admit when you're wrong. I just hope Jim and I never get like the two of you! I want our marriage to last."

Deciding to put an end to this ridiculous conversation, Tessa pulled the cell phone from her purse to follow up on her car's problem. After a brief call to the mechanic, she took up her purse and headed for the door. "Carl towed my car to his garage. It was the solenoid just as he'd suspected. He has it fixed, and one of his staff is coming after me. I told him I'd be waiting out front."

Katie struggled to her feet then gently grabbed her mother's arm. "I'm sorry, Mom. I didn't mean to be so smart-mouthed. I—I hope you'll forgive me."

Tessa cupped her daughter's hand and gave it a squeeze. "Forgive you for what? Being honest? Or for speaking from your heart?"

The two women smiled at one another. Tessa kissed Katie's cheek then headed for the door. "I'll be home if you need me. Love you."

ɤ

Mike glanced at his watch as he stood on Tessa's front porch. Seven thirty. He knew she was there. Katie had told him Carl had repaired her car, and it was parked in the driveway.

Maybe he should have called first instead of just turning up on her doorstep uninvited. No, he was already there. He'd just take his chances and hope she'd cooled off and wouldn't rail at him for not being available when she'd needed him.

He pushed the doorbell button and waited.

Tessa pulled open the door and eyed him suspiciously. "Well, look who's here."

Nope, she hasn't cooled off. She's still mad. He forced a smile. "Hi. Had supper yet?"

She merely gave him a vacant stare.

"I really am sorry about this morning, Tessie. Katie told me Carl got your car running and that you had taken care of the dress problem. I figured you'd had a pretty rotten day and the least I could do was take you out to supper."

She tilted her head to one side and stared at him. "I promised myself and Katie I wasn't going to get upset about this."

He ventured a grin. "Then you'll let me take you to supper?"

"If you'll do something for me."

"Anything within my power. Just name it."

Tessa presented him with a challenging smile. "Go to church with me in the morning."

Go to church with her? He certainly hadn't expected that to be her request. "I—I guess I could do that," he answered reluctantly, hoping to make peace between them. "I haven't been for a long time."

Tessa's smile broadened. "Good. I'll count on it. Give me a second to lock up and get my purse."

Both relieved and surprised by their docile conversation, since he had expected a tirade when he arrived, he nodded. "I'll wait in the car."

❧

"And that's what happened with the dress. Pure carelessness on the part of the delivery boy and poor Katie went into a tailspin," she told him as they sat at the corner booth in their favorite little Mexican restaurant. "Let's hope nothing else happens to our daughter before this wedding is over. I'm not sure she or Jim could handle another problem."

"Yeah, I agree." Mike stared into his cup as he stirred his coffee. "I'm really glad to see those two are getting married. I've hated that they were living together."

"Me, too. I did my best to talk Katie out of it, but our stubborn daughter wouldn't listen to a word."

Mike felt her hand touch his. He wished she'd ask him about the two important cases he was working on, show some interest in his work, but she didn't. He needed to talk to her about it and its importance to the community, to share the highs and lows of police work, like he had done those first few years after they'd married.

"You will make it to the rehearsal dinner and the wedding, won't you?"

"Look, Tessie. As I've told you, these two cases are really important ones. Two of the most important I've ever worked." His free hand cupped hers, and he gave her a smile. "But I'll be there. I promise."

After lingering over a final cup of coffee, Mike drove Tessa home. He'd barely climbed back into his car when his cell phone rang. He listened, grinned, then hung up as he hit the car's accelerator and raced toward the lower east side. Finally, he had the lead he'd been hoping for.

eight

Deciding to retire early for a change, Tessa donned her nightgown, propped the pillows up against the headboard, grabbed the TV remote, and crawled into bed. The ten o'clock news was just beginning.

"A little less than an hour ago, little three-month-old Marilee Carter, who had been kidnapped from her crib as she lay sleeping in the room next to her parents, was found alive and well, thanks to the dogged pursuit and intense investigation of one of San Diego's longtime detectives. Detective Mike Garrett had promised Mr. and Mrs. Mark Carter he would not rest until he found their precious little girl, and Detective Garrett did just that. By working round the clock and following up on hundreds of leads, tonight Detective Garrett was able to apprehend the young woman who had kidnapped little Marilee and reunite the child with her joyful parents. When questioned, twenty-eight-year-old unemployed waitress, Margaret Peterson, admitted she had planned to pass Marilee Carter off as her own daughter and sell her to a desperate couple who had advertised in the newspaper for a baby."

Tessa sat glued to the spot, unable to believe what she was hearing. Mike—her Mike—had brought that family back together? That's why he'd gotten all those phone calls? Had to duck out on her all those times?

"When asked why this case was so important to him," the news anchor continued, "Detective Garrett said, and I quote,

'I have a daughter myself. I can't imagine ever being separated from her. Nothing is more important than family. I determined I was going to follow up on every lead, regardless of how insignificant it was, until I located the Carters' baby.' And Detective Garrett and the San Diego Police Department did just that. I also asked Detective Garrett if he ever doubted they'd find the child alive. This was his response. Again, I quote. 'In a kidnapping case,' he said, 'time is of the essence. Fortunately, we were able to find and return little Marilee to her parents alive and well. Not all infant kidnappings turn out that way. Just seeing the joy on her parents' faces made all the hours of searching for Marilee worth the time and effort we put in.' Because of dedicated men like Detective Mike Garrett," the announcer said, smiling into the camera, "little Marilee Carter is sleeping in her own bed tonight, safe and sound."

"Mike! Why didn't you tell me?" Already knowing the answer, Tessa shuddered. "Because you thought I didn't want to hear, and you were right. I've been too caught up in my own selfish little world to even think about what your life was like."

A tear trickled down her cheek as a short video clip ran of Mr. and Mrs. Carter weeping as they cuddled and kissed their adorable baby. "No wonder you get such satisfaction out of your job, and I didn't even care enough to ask you about it or understand why you would suddenly take off when you got a phone call. How callous you must think I am."

Her heart racing, she reached for the phone. "Mike, I was watching the news about little Marilee. I—I just wanted to congratulate you," she told him when he answered. "What a thrill it must have been to find that child."

"Thanks, Tessie. It was pretty exciting, all right." From the tone of his voice it was obvious he hadn't expected a call from her, especially a congratulatory one.

"I—I'm very proud of you."

"You are?"

She swallowed at her pride. "From what the newscaster said, without you, the Carters may never have found their baby."

"I got lucky. I had a hunch that baby was going to be sold so I followed a few leads, called in a few markers and, praise God, found that little girl before something dreadful happened to her. Fortunately, her kidnapper took good care of her."

Did Mike say "praise God"? Perhaps he wasn't as far from God as he appeared. A chill ran down Tessa's spine when she considered what might have happened if Mike hadn't been so persistent in his pursuit of that child. "You're a hero, Mike."

He huffed. "All in a day's work, Tessie, all in a day's work."

"Well, I don't care what you say. You're a hero in my eyes."

"You have no idea what it means to me to hear you say that."

Gripping the phone tightly, she whispered softly, "I—I should have said it long ago."

There was a pause on the other end, as if her words had rendered him speechless. "I—I'll see you in the morning. About ten? I figured you'd want to go to the late service."

Tessa's heart leaped. Mike was still planning on going to church with her. "Ten is fine. Congratulations again. Good night."

"Night, Tessie, and thanks for calling."

She lay in bed, alone in the dark for a long time, ashamed to think she'd let her own petty needs take priority above that of an innocent child. But how could she have known? He never mentioned the missing child.

The reason hit her right between the eyes, jolting her into reality. He had failed to mention the missing child or any of his other cases because, other than their first couple of years together, she'd never shown one iota of interest in his work as a detective. Now she began to understand why he couldn't give it up.

As promised, Mike rang the doorbell at exactly ten the next morning. Though heads turned as the two of them entered the sanctuary of Granite Hills Seaside Community Church neither she nor Mike took notice. Tessa led him to a front pew—the pew he and Tessa and Katie had claimed as their own the first day they'd visited that church.

Both Ellen and Bill, who were seated directly behind them, smiled and greeted them warmly, as did other members of the congregation. To Tessa's delight, Mike joined in the singing and even read along when Pastor McIntosh led in a responsive reading of the Scripture. She loved hearing Mike's deep husky voice. How she'd missed it. A pang of joy swept over her as their shoulders touched and Mike smiled at her.

❧

Mike stole a glance at Tessa. How long had it been since they'd sat together in a church service? How long since they'd felt comfortable in each other's presence?

He'd forgotten how beautiful she was. Maybe the ugly words they'd had over the years had masked her beauty and made him forget how much he loved her.

He scooted a tad closer and gently, fearfully, took her hand, afraid she might pull away from him. Instead she, ever so slightly, leaned into him. How lonely he'd been. How he'd missed the closeness they'd once shared. A pleasant, familiar fragrance jarred his senses. Was that the same perfume he'd bought her for Christmas those first few years they were married?

The offering taken and the choir's special number sung, Pastor McIntosh moved to the podium and after a lighthearted anecdote began his sermon. Mike tried to avoid listening as Pastor McIntosh told of the prodigal son who had wandered away from his father, cutting all ties, but he couldn't. The message seemed to be aimed directly at him, striking a too-long dormant, unresponsive chord in his heart.

"It makes no difference how far you've wandered from God, or how many times you've turned your back on Him." Pastor McIntosh paused, his gaze sweeping the vast audience of listeners. "He's there, waiting to forgive you. God longs to have fellowship with you, to walk with you when the storms of life beat you down. Forget your foolish pride. God knows the thoughts, the desires, and the intents of your heart. Surrender. Turn it all over to Him. Ask the forgiveness of the only One who can truly forgive. Oh, wandering soul—return to the God who loves you."

Deeply touched, Mike clamped his eyes shut and gulped hard. Wandering soul. Those two simple words described the life he'd lived for so many years he'd dared not count them.

Pastor McIntosh held his arms open wide as he moved down the carpeted steps from the podium. "Return to the God who loves you. Return to the God who cares. Only God can straighten out the mess we make of our lives. God can forgive you when you can't forgive yourself. Cast your burden upon Him. Give Him your life—your all."

It was all Mike could do to hold himself in the pew. He wanted to run to the front and kneel at the altar. *My life is a mess—a mess I created.* He fidgeted uncomfortably in his seat as the choir sang a hymn of invitation.

"We're going to sing one more verse. Don't let this opportunity to make things right with God pass you by." Pastor McIntosh bowed his head low and stood silently waiting.

Mike wanted to steal a look at Tessie. Was she looking at

him? The pressure he felt to respond to the pastor's invitation was overwhelming. His hands fiercely gripped the top of the pew in front of him as a battle raged inside. Were those beads of sweat he felt on his forehead?

"If you've felt God's call today and you haven't made the decision to accept Him and His forgiveness, remember, you don't have to be in a church to commune with the Heavenly Father. He's ready to listen to you anytime, anywhere, on your turf or His."

Mike's hold on the pew relaxed. The altar call was over. But try as he may to put it out of his mind, the almost overpowering urge to confess his sins and ask God's forgiveness remained long after the pastor had said the benediction and the congregation filed out.

"Good to see you here," Bill Zobel told him, shaking his hand vigorously when the two met in the parking lot as Mike was closing Tessa's door.

Though still shaken by the morning's message, Mike uttered a friendly, "Yeah, nice to be here. Good to see you, Bill."

Smiling, Bill placed his hand on Mike's shoulder. "You know, Mike, it's been way too long since you and I have had a good round of golf. I've missed our times together. As soon as Katie's wedding is over let's hit the greens and lose a few balls. Whatcha say?"

Mike returned his smile. "I'd like that, Bill. Let's do it."

Tessa was fastening her seat belt and smiled up at him as Mike climbed into the car. "Great message, wasn't it?"

He nodded, Pastor McIntosh's words still ringing in his ears.

"I–I'm so glad you came with me, Mike."

He cast a quick glance in her direction. She was smiling at him like the old Tessa had smiled at him, and he found himself in awe of her beauty. "Thanks for inviting me," he said simply, not wanting her to know the turmoil that had been going on in his soul. "I've always liked Pastor McIntosh. He's a good guy."

Before she could respond or mention anything else about the morning's sermon, he headed the car across the lot and onto the street. "You are going to let me take you to lunch, aren't you?"

She let loose a giggle that sent his heart reeling. "I was hoping you'd ask."

☙

Tessa couldn't contain her grin as the hostess seated them at a cozy table for two in the beautifully decorated restaurant. She and Mike, together—attending church, having lunch, being civil to one another—something she'd doubted would ever happen again in their lifetime.

"What?" Mike asked, reaching across the table to cup her hand in his as they pushed away their dessert plates and the waitress poured each of them a final cup of coffee.

Her smile broadened. "What, what?"

"I just wondered what you were thinking about."

She felt his grip tighten and knew she must be blushing. "You. Me. Us together. That's all."

"Yeah. This is like old times. I kinda like it. How about you?"

Tessa gazed at this handsome, though somewhat older and a bit stockier man who, at one time, she had loved and pledged her life to. *Be still, my heart. Remember—nothing has changed except that the two of you have called a temporary truce until after Katie's wedding. Once it's over, he'll go back to being the same old Mike. Never there when you need him. Always at the beck and call of some murder scene, robbery, missing person, and on and on and on. You can't open up yourself for hurt again just because he's performed heroic deeds and taken up temporary residence in your life. It's too painful. You can't go through that again. You haven't even recovered from the first time.*

"Tessie? Did you hear me?"

His deep, husky voice jolted her back to her senses, sending up her shield of protection between them. "Yes, I heard you, Mike, and I agree it is somewhat like old times but—"

"Hello, you two. What a nice surprise!"

Both Tessa and Mike turned toward the voice. It was Gina Alexander, Mike's former partner and friend of many years who had retired from the police force and moved to Washington.

"I'm so glad to see the both of you together," the woman went on. "Some of our friends at the police station told me you had broken up."

With a slump of his normally broad square shoulders, Mike nodded. "We are still separated, Gina."

"We've been helping our daughter plan her wedding," Tessa added, smiling. She'd liked Gina and had been glad when she'd been assigned as Mike's partner. "It's really good to see you again."

"Mike was the best partner I ever had," Gina said, her hand clamping his shoulder affectionately. "Partners develop a close relationship. Learn to trust each other. Sometimes our lives depend on that trust. That's the way it was with me and Mike. We were a great team." She smiled at Tessa. "He'll probably be furious with me for telling you, but Mike confided in me about some of the things that were causing trouble in your marriage. Believe me, all married cops have the same problem. You weren't unique. Spouses never understand our dedication to our jobs. Not even my dear husband, God rest his soul."

Tessa gasped. "You lost Kirk?"

Gina nodded, her eyes filling with tears. "Yes, just two months ago. Life will never be the same without him."

"Oh, Gina, I'm so sorry," Tessa told her, reaching out to cup Gina's wrist. "I didn't know."

"Me, either," Mike said, shaking his head sadly. "I liked Kirk. I know you miss him."

"I do," Gina said, her voice quivering. "Sometimes we don't know what we have until we lose it." Turning her full attention to Tessa, she added, "You're a lucky woman, Tessa Garrett, whether you realize it or not. Mike is a good man, and he loves you. I know you and Mike are Christians and you know the power of God's forgiveness. You can't continue to let something that happened many years ago keep you two apart. You belong together."

Tessa's mind was a whir. "But—"

"I know it's none of my business," Gina added, looking from one to the other, "but it grieves me to see two people who were meant for each other separate because of foolish pride. Life is short. Whatever is keeping you apart is not worth the effort." With a smile she backed away and blew them each a kiss. "Take this lonely woman's advice. Kiss and make up. You'll be glad you did."

Before they could respond, she disappeared into the crowd of Sunday diners.

Mike sat at the table, his hands cradling his empty coffee cup. Tessa could tell Gina's words were niggling at his mind. They were niggling at hers, too. *How could I have been so blind? So selfish? Because of my arrogant refusal to compromise, I lost the most precious thing in my life. Mike. The husband I loved dearly.*

Clutching her purse to her chest, Tessa rose. "I–I'm sorry, Mike. I need to be alone." She hurried away from the table before he could rise and try to stop her. Swallowing her pride, she rushed toward the maître d' and instructed him to call her a taxi and ask them to come quickly, then hurried outside. Having to face Mike right now, after hearing Gina's words, was more than she could handle. *I've got to be alone, to pray and talk to my Heavenly Father. Only He understands me and knows how I feel.*

≈

Mike was touched by Gina's words. He waited for what seemed an eternity then, concerned about Tessa and unable to stand being separated from her any longer, hurried toward the ladies' room where he was sure she had gone.

"There was no one in there but me," a kindly lady told him as she exited the restroom. He thanked the woman, then leaned awkwardly against the wall, not sure what to do next. Where could Tessa be? In the lobby? Maybe out by his car? "I've got to find her."

≈

Tessa had barely arrived home from the restaurant and flung herself across the bed before Mike had appeared on her porch, shouting her name and ringing the doorbell over and over until she thought she would scream. Didn't he realize she didn't want to talk to him now?

When he finally gave up and she heard his car back out of the driveway, she dropped to her knees by her bed and called out to her heavenly Father. Soon Mike's persistent phone calls began, and she found it difficult to even concentrate. Finally, she could stand it no longer. With her heart pounding in her ears, she lifted the phone, shut off the ringer, and clicked off the lamp. If there were a dire emergency, Katie would call Tessa's cell phone, which was still on and inside her purse atop the dresser.

After a fitful night of turning and tossing and praying, Tessa crawled out of bed, her makeup still on, her hair disheveled, and her mouth tasting like her teeth hadn't been brushed in days. It took only one look in the mirror, and all she wanted to do was crawl back in bed and pull the covers over her head. Where was the comfort God was supposed to give when you called out to Him? She was as miserable now as she'd been when she'd raced out of that restaurant.

Eventually, she forced herself out of bed, stumbled toward the window, and pulled the curtain aside, half expecting to find Mike's car in the driveway, but it wasn't there. *Oh, Mike, what have I done?*

Suddenly remembering the wedding rehearsal and dinner was today, she hurriedly dialed Katie's number.

"Hi, Mom. What's up?" Katie's cheery voice answered.

"I—I just wondered if there were any last-minute things you wanted me to do today," Tessa answered, trying to sound upbeat. The last thing she wanted was to upset her daughter. "Do you want me to call the caterer and make sure he has everything set up like you'd planned it?"

"I got up early and went over my list. I've already made a few calls. I'm going to call him as soon as I finish talking with you. I think everything is taken care of. You and Daddy have done a fabulous job of pinch-hitting for me. I can't thank you enough." Katie let out a slight giggle. "Do you realize in just two days I'll be a married woman? Mrs. James Martinez. I'm so glad we decided to go ahead with the wedding, but we couldn't have pulled it off without the two of you."

"I've loved helping you. How's the ankle doing?"

"The doc said I'm doing great. The break is healing well and even though I'll have to wear the strap-on cast, I'll be able to stand at my wedding with no trouble at all and, hopefully, the cast won't even be noticeable."

"That's wonderful news, Katie. I'm glad to hear you're doing so well."

"Oh, by the way, Mom, I tried to call you last night, but

your line just rang, and the answering machine didn't pick up. Was something wrong with it?"

"No, I shut the ringer off and went to bed. The answering machine must be full of messages I should delete." Tessa didn't bother to mention they were all from Katie's father.

"It wasn't urgent. I was just calling to tell you that Jim had to fly to Kansas City yesterday to meet with the CEO of one of his major accounts, but he'll be back in plenty of time for the wedding rehearsal and dinner tonight."

Tessa sat down on the edge of the bed and leaned back against the pillows, the back of her hand resting across her forehead. "Oh, sweetie, did he have to go? Couldn't someone have gone in his place?"

Katie laughed. "Don't be such a worrier, Mom. Of course he had to go, but he's catching an early afternoon flight. That client always insists on Jim's personal attention. They're negotiating some big deal. He'll be back in San Diego by four o'clock."

"But tonight's such a special night for you. Couldn't they have put it off until after the first of the year?"

"Mom! Jim would never have gone if he didn't think it was necessary. You know that."

Tessa sighed. "I guess you're right."

"You are still planning to open the church for the caterer this afternoon, aren't you?"

"Yes, I plan to be there by three thirty."

"Thanks, Mom. Oh, I've been meaning to ask—how did it go with Daddy yesterday? We went to the early service with Valene and Jordan since Jim was taking a noon flight so we missed seeing you. Did he go to church with you like he said he would?"

Tessa felt her pulse quicken. "Yes, he made it. We had lunch afterward; then I—I came on home."

"That's it?" Katie sounded disappointed. "I'd hoped the two of you would spend the afternoon together."

"No. I—I had things to do, and I'm sure he did, too."

"Well, I'd better let you go so I can call the caterer. I'll remind them you'll have the church open by three thirty. I love you, Mom."

"I love you, too, sweetie."

Tessa cleared Mike's phone messages as soon as she hung up. Although the phone rang a number of times during the day, she let the answering machine pick up. With the exception of two calls from Ellen and one from Pastor McIntosh, all of the calls were from Mike. "I really need to talk to you, Tessie," he'd say, a distinct air of concern in his voice. "Please pick up if you're there, or call me when you get home."

But she didn't. Her mind was in far too much turmoil.

She was just leaving the house at three when the phone rang again. Thinking perhaps it was another call from Ellen she paused in the doorway and listened. But it wasn't Ellen; it was Katie.

"Hi, Mom." Katie's voice sounded strange. "I'm afraid I have bad news. Jim's flight has been grounded. They're having an ice storm in Kansas City. There's no way he's going to make it in time for the rehearsal and dinner."

Leaving the door standing open, Tessa raced for the phone. "Katie, don't hang up! I'm here! What are you going to do?"

"Oh, Mom, there's not much I can do, but go ahead as planned. Jim is sick about missing the dinner. He suggested Daddy stand in for him at the rehearsal; then he can fill Jim in on the routine when he gets back. Jim phoned again a few minutes ago and said the storm is letting up some and the forecast for tomorrow is good. If his flight doesn't make it out tonight, at least he'll be out tomorrow morning."

Tessa dropped her purse onto the sofa then sank down beside it. "Oh, honey, I'm so sorry."

"Me, too, but there is nothing we can do but, as Jim says, go on without him. The important thing is that he gets back safely."

"I'll open the church then come after you."

"No, that's okay. Daddy stopped by on his way to the station. He's offered to pick me up."

Tessa huffed. "You'd better pray he makes it."

"Mom! Would you please try to go at least one day without bad-mouthing Daddy? For my sake?"

Hating herself for being so judgmental, Tessa bit her lip. "I'll try."

Tessa stayed at the church the rest of the afternoon, assisting the caterer and his team when needed. The remainder of the time she spent tying the satin bows that would be hung at the ends of the pews for Katie and Jim's Christmas Day wedding.

"Phone for you, Tessa," Mary Margaret Hughes, Pastor McIntosh's secretary, called to her from across the dining room thirty minutes before time for the dinner to begin. "It's Katie. She said it's important."

Tessa rushed to the woman's office and grabbed up the phone. "What's wrong?"

"Dad just called. He's going to be late. Can you come after me?"

Her anger rising, Tessa ground out, "I knew we couldn't depend on him. What is it? Another big case only he can handle?"

"He didn't say, Mom. Just that he was running late. Can you come, or should I call someone else?"

"I'll be there in a few minutes."

They arrived at the church just in time for the dinner to begin. Pastor McIntosh prayed for their meal, for Katie and Jim as they prepared for their marriage, and for Jim's safety and quick return. With Katie and Tessa leading them, the line of attendees moved through the magnificent buffet line the caterer had prepared, oohing and aahing at the vast array of attractively prepared food, filling their plates to overflowing.

Though miffed at Mike for letting Katie down, Tessa did her best to enjoy the food and appear cheerful. The caterer was already clearing the serving table when Mike appeared in the doorway, a bandage across his forehead.

nine

Katie rose from her place at the head table and hurried toward him, deep concern etched on her face. "Daddy! What happened to you?"

Mike put his arm around her and pulled her to him. "Don't worry about it, pumpkin. I'm okay. It's merely a surface wound."

Katie lifted worried eyes. "It doesn't look like it."

Tucking a finger under his daughter's chin, Mike lifted her gaze to meet his. "I had a little trouble with a suspect I was arresting. That's all. The doc said I could take the bandage off tomorrow. I'm really sorry I missed your rehearsal dinner."

"I'm just glad you're here now." Katie turned to Tessa. "Mom, would you get the plate I asked the caterer to save for Daddy?"

While avoiding Mike's gaze, Tessa forced a smile for Katie's sake. "Sure, honey. Be glad to." While everyone fussed over Mike, Tessa fetched his plate from the kitchen then set it down on the table in front of him without a word, though inwardly she was as concerned about his injury as everyone else was.

Mike grabbed her hand before she could get away, his gaze locking with hers. "Thanks, Tessie. I've been trying to call you."

Not wanting to appear rude in front of their friends, Tessa managed a slight smile. "I—I've been busy. Last-minute things to take care of, you know."

Pastor McIntosh took charge when the wedding party gathered in the sanctuary at seven o'clock for the rehearsal. "Since Jim has been detained in Kansas City due to an ice storm, he has asked Mike to stand in for him as the groom."

148

Before the attendants walked down the aisle, Mike hurried to the platform and took the place Jim should have taken—next to where Jordan, his best man, and Nathan and Brandon, his groomsmen, would soon be standing.

Moments later, with the attendants now flanking the bride and substitute groom, Jordan gave Mike a mischievous smile. "Hey, *Jim*, you've put on a bit of weight, haven't you?"

Mike responded with a wink. "You, Brandon, and Nathan better hope you're in as good of shape as I am when you're my age. Just ask that perp I arrested this evening. He's sitting in a jail cell right now, thanks to this old guy and his agility."

"We have another substitution," Pastor McIntosh said, grinning at Mike's comment. "Since Mike is tied up pretending he is the groom, Bill Zobel is going to stand in as the father of the bride and walk Katie down the aisle."

"Don't forget," Katie reminded him. "I want both Dad and Mom to give me away."

"I was just about to add that, Katie. I think it's a lovely idea." After a few more comments and instructions, Pastor McIntosh motioned to the organist and the strains of the wedding march filled the sanctuary. He nodded toward Bill Zobel and Katie and her attendants. "Slowly now, walk slowly. This is your time, Katie. Everyone wants a good look at the bride."

When they reached the altar, Pastor McIntosh asked, "Who gives this woman to be married to this man?"

Tessa rose and stood beside Bill. Gazing at her beautiful daughter, Tessa couldn't hold back her tears of joy.

With an oversized grin toward Mike, Bill answered, "Her mother and I do," as the entire wedding party muffled giggles and Bill led Tessa back to her seat.

When the laughter subsided, Pastor McIntosh instructed Mike and Katie to move close together and hold hands.

"Jane and Keene will sing their duet here," Pastor McIntosh said, nodding toward the Morays.

"I just want you to know, Katie," Keene said, smiling as he reached out and took her hand, "it's an honor to sing at your wedding. I just hope you and Jim can be every bit as happy as Jane and I are. Keep God first in your life and all will be well."

Jane nodded as she slipped her arm around her husband's shoulders. "He's right, Katie. God needs to be the center of your home."

"He's going to be the center of our home, Jane. Jim and I have already decided that."

Keene gave her a thumbs-up. "Then you two are on the right track."

"I'm really glad you weren't out on one of your concert tours, Keene," Mike added, "so you two could be a part of our Katie's wedding. She looks up to both of you."

"We wouldn't have missed it." Jane sent a smile Katie's way. "Katie and Jim are two very special people. We want only the best for them."

"I know Keene and Jane's duet will touch hearts. I've heard them rehearsing," Pastor McIntosh said. "You'll love the words. They're right out of the scriptures." He motioned toward Katie. "Katie, while Jane and Keene are singing, you and Mike hold hands and gaze into each other's eyes, like you and Jim will be doing during the actual ceremony."

The two moved into place.

"Now," the pastor said, "when their lovely duet ends, you both need to face me, and I want you to continue to hold hands. I will be reading some scripture here; then I will give the short sermon I always give before I perform the actual wedding ceremony. I'm going to do that tonight so you'll get a feel for what I have in mind, but I'll try to keep it fairly brief since this is only the rehearsal. Remember, some in your group of friends, family, and coworkers attending your wedding may not know the Lord. We want to give them the opportunity to hear what God's Word says about accepting Him." He glanced toward Katie. "How you doing, Katie? You seem a little tired. Think you can stand awhile longer?"

Katie frowned and let out a sigh. "Actually, Pastor McIntosh, I really am tired. I've been on my feet most of the day taking care of last-minute details, and this cast is so uncomfortable. Maybe I should sit down for a while."

"That's probably a good idea," he told her, showing great concern. "But we'll need someone to stand in your place so everyone will know what to do and when to do it during the actual ceremony."

Katie turned to Tessa. "Would you stand in for me, Mom?"

"M—me?" Tessa stammered, totally caught off guard by Katie's surprising request.

"Please, Mom. I'd really appreciate it. I need to get off my feet."

After casting a quick glance toward Mike, then at the pastor, Tessa nodded and rose. "Sure. I guess I can, if you're sure you want me to, but maybe Vanessa or—"

"Please, Mom. I'd feel better if you did it." Katie, with Mike's assistance, moved down the steps from the platform. "I'll watch from your place, that way I can prop my foot up on the pew."

Feeling a flush rise to her cheeks, Tessa made sure Katie was seated then joined Mike at the altar.

Pastor McIntosh looked from one to the other. "Good. Now we're ready. Let's proceed."

Tessa moved next to Mike and flinched slightly when she felt his fingers entwine with hers. Just the touch of his hand sent shivers down her spine. Her mind flashed to another time—years ago—when she and Mike had stood before the altar holding hands. How young they were then, and so much in love. She gulped hard. Her grandmother's and grandfather's words, said many years ago, filled her mind and made her wish she'd taken their advice. If she had, perhaps things would have been different.

"Tessa," her grandmother had said, "you must be sure you're making the right decision and that God is leading you and Mike together. God doesn't look lightly on marriage, nor does He accept any excuse for a husband and wife to separate. When you marry Mike, it will be until death do the two of you part. If you have any doubts—"

"But I don't have doubts," she had told her grandmother. "I love Mike. I'll always love him. Nothing will ever be able to separate us."

Her grandfather had reminded her, "God must always be first in your home, and you must respect your husband, Tessa. You may not always agree with him, but you must respect him and his decisions. A good marriage takes work. Hard work. There will be times you'll want to throw in the towel, give up, but you must never do it. Mark my words, Tessa, true love is worth finding but—more importantly—true love is worth keeping. When you pledge your life to Mike, before God and your friends, that pledge is for a lifetime. There's no turning back."

But, Granddad, Tessa whispered within her heart. *I tried, Granddad. Honest, I did. It just wouldn't work. You know that. You've seen how Mike has pulled away from me, putting his work and everything else before me and Katie. I couldn't live that way. Living with Mike was impossible!*

Tessa ventured a glance toward the handsome man holding her hand and found him gazing at her. Though she tried with all her might to hold it back, a slight smile played at her lips. Who was she kidding? She'd never stopped loving Mike. She'd only tried to convince herself she had. Was she blushing? She hoped not. Turning away, she looked in Katie's direction and found her daughter's attention focused on the two of them. Had Katie planned this? Was this another of her sly little ways of trying to get them back together?

ﾊ

Mike tightened his grip on Tessa's hand and was surprised when she didn't pull away. *Oh, Tessie—if only we could turn back the clock, become the naïve young people we were when you and I said our I dos. Where did we go wrong, babe? Was my career as a police officer worth separating myself from my family like I did? I'll be retiring before too many more years. What will I have to show for the time I spent away from you and Katie? A gold watch? A decent retirement check? A lonely apartment?*

" 'Love is patient, love is kind. It does not envy, it does not boast, it is not proud,' " Pastor McIntosh quoted. "Most folks search for true love all their life—some find it but never realize what they have is exactly what they've been searching for. They refuse to compromise and seek a common ground acceptable to both parties. True love rarely runs smoothly, but—at the end of the day—when lovers come together, they have one another to count on, to encourage, to share their joys and sorrows. When you find that kind of love, hold on to it. Cherish it. Nourish it, because true love between a husband and wife is worth keeping."

Mike glanced Tessa's way and found her gazing at him. What was it he saw in her eyes? Not the hatred or ridicule he'd expected to find. Nor the I-don't-care look she gave him so often. No, this look was kind, gentle—maybe even—dare he think it? Loving? The way she used to look at him before the humdrum daily routine of life took over and they went their separate ways?

*Oh, Tessie—dear, dear Tessie. You'll always be the girl I love. The girl
I married. I thought our love was so strong nothing could ever tear us
apart. If only you could forgive me—if only it wasn't too—*

"Love can be an elusive thing. You think it is within your
grasp, never to escape from you, and then, poof! Something
happens, and the love you thought you had for that other
person, your better half, begins to dwindle. They're no longer
the wonderful person you thought you married. Sometimes
you even find yourself avoiding one another. Other people
take over the role as confidant, encourager, and the one they
turn to, and you're hurt. You feel deserted. Alone. Maybe
you seek the companionship of others. You feel righteous
indignation. How dare your partner treat you like that?" He
paused, his look scanning the audience, and then resting on
Mike and Tessa. "But was the other person totally responsible
for the failure of that marriage? Or does the fault and blame
lie with both parties? What is the missing ingredient in that
marriage? The glue that holds it together?"

Every eye was fixed on Pastor McIntosh as he dramatically
paused again, the silence deafening. The beat of Mike's heart
pounded in his ears.

"God. He's the glue. The *super* glue that never fails. When two
people begin to leave Him out of their relationship, their love for
each other can begin to wane. God wants to be the foundation of
every marriage. The glue that binds the couple together."

With a look of tenderness, Pastor McIntosh reached out and
took Mike's and Tessa's hands in his. "At this point, if Katie
and Jim were standing before me instead of Mike and Tessa,
I would ask them to look each other in the eye and declare
their love for one another by reciting the vows they've written.
But, even though I have a copy of those vows, we'll omit them
tonight. The vows they've written are very personal. They'd

best be held until the service."

Mike blinked hard. His heart touched deeply as Pastor McIntosh's words replayed in his thoughts. *"When you find that kind of love, hold on to it. Cherish it. Nourish it, because true love between a husband and wife is worth keeping." Why didn't I realize that? Why didn't I do everything in my power to be the husband and father I should have been? I was a fool, such a fool.* He lifted his eyes heavenward. *God, is it too late? Can even You put our family back together again?* He gave Tessa's hand a slight squeeze. How he needed her in his life. How he loved her.

Pastor McIntosh led them through the rest of the service, pausing and repeating instructions where necessary, then said, "This is where I will say, 'By the power invested in me by the State of California, I now pronounce you Husband and Wife.' And I'd say, 'You may kiss the bride.' "

On impulse, and feeling very nostalgic as he remembered his own wedding, Mike grabbed Tessa up in his arms and planted a kiss on her lips, a kiss much like he'd given her on their wedding day.

Hoots and hollers sounded from the wedding party.

"Hey, Mike—way to go!" Jordan chided as he led the audience in an impromptu applause. "Looks like the old guy has still got it!"

But Mike's attention wasn't on those who were cheering him on, or the pastor, or anyone else. His attention was centered on the lovely woman in his arms, and he never wanted to let her go.

Placing her hands on his chest, Tessa tried to push herself away, a look of shock blanketing her face.

"Hey, what's going on here?"

All eyes turned toward the door. It was Jim. He'd made it back from Kansas City, safe and sound. The wedding rehearsal was over.

Mike's heart sank as Tessa and the others rushed toward Jim, leaving him and the pastor alone at the altar. He hoped Tessa wasn't mad at him for his impulsive behavior, but even if she was, the kiss was worth it. He'd wanted to kiss her like that, really kiss her, since they'd first begun working together on Katie's wedding. The opportunity had presented itself, and he'd seized it.

"You really love Tessa, don't you, Mike?"

Startled, Mike looked up into Pastor McIntosh's kind eyes. "It's that obvious, huh?"

"You two vowed before God to love and cherish each other until death. God wants you together, Mike. You've not only left Tessie, you've left God. Isn't it about time you did what you could to make amends with both of them?"

Mike hung his head dejectedly. "I'm afraid it's too late."

"It's never too late. God is always ready to hear the prayers and confessions of His children. And Tessa? Though her heart has been deeply wounded, she still loves you, Mike. I know she does." He placed a hand on Mike's shoulder. "If I were you, I'd set things right with God, then I'd go after that sweet lady. Tell her how much you love her and want to put your marriage back together. If you love her like I think you do, it's worth a try, isn't it?"

Mike thought about his words then nodded. "I'll do it."

By the time he finished talking to Pastor McIntosh, Tessa's car was moving out of the parking lot. Mike waited until she pulled into the line of traffic then followed her, keeping a few cars between them. He turned in behind her when she pulled into her driveway, leaped out of his car, and rushed to open her door for her. "I was hoping you'd invite me in for a cup of coffee," he told her, half expecting her to reach out and slap his face for his impulsive kiss at the rehearsal.

❧

Tessa stared at Mike, not sure how she should respond. Though he'd definitely stepped over the line when he'd kissed her, she had to admit she'd enjoyed it. "Sure. I guess. Come on in." She moved quickly toward the door, key ring in hand. "I think we could both use a cup of coffee."

Tessa motioned Mike toward his old recliner chair then moved quickly into the kitchen to start the coffee maker. When the coffee finished dripping, she filled two mugs with the hot, brown liquid and carried them into the family room, handing one to Mike before settling herself on the sofa.

"Thanks," Mike said simply, eyeing her as she placed her cup on the coffee table.

"You're welcome."

Mike set his cup on the end table then leaned forward, resting his elbows on his knees. "I'd say I'm sorry for kissing you in front of everyone like that, Tessie, but I'm not. I've wanted to kiss you since—"

"No harm done," Tessa said, shrugging her shoulders and doing her best to appear nonchalant. "You were just caught up in the moment."

Mike rose and joined her on the sofa. "No! That wasn't it at all, Tessie. I kissed you because I love you. Pastor McIntosh and I talked about it at the church. He encouraged me to try to set things right with you and with God."

He seemed sincere enough, but hadn't he seemed sincere hundreds of times before when he'd told her he loved her and was going to spend more time with her, and with Katie? And hadn't he forgotten those words in a matter of days? Going back to his old routine of working round the clock? Letting anything and everything take him away from his family?

"Mike," she said softly, trying to keep her composure and

not cry, "I appreciate what you're saying, and I do hope you get yourself straightened out with God, but so much has happened between us. Things I find hard to forget."

"You mean forgive, don't you? Why can't you forgive me, Tessie? Is it that you don't want to forgive me? Do you enjoy being the martyr?"

Though offended, his words caused her to examine her heart. "I want to forgive you, Mike. Really I do. These past two weeks have made me see you in a different light. I've loved every minute I've had with you but—"

"I will put you first, Tessie. I'm a new man. Being with you these past two weeks has made me see what I've missed. I—"

His cell phone rang, and though he didn't answer it immediately, he finally snatched it from his belt. "Garrett," he barked into it impatiently.

Tessa watched with annoyance as he listened and scribbled a few notes on the pad he'd pulled from his pocket.

"You're sure? Absolutely sure? Because if this is a wild-goose chase, I don't—" He nodded. "Right. Gotcha. I'll be right there."

While Tessa watched, her dander rising, Mike shoved the phone back into its belt clip and reached for her hand.

"I'm sorry, babe. That call was really important. I've got to go. We've got the best lead we've had yet in the murder that happened at the Fairbanks Mall last week."

Rejecting his hand, Tessa rolled her eyes. "Go on, Mike. You have a job to do. You can't put me first, in spite of what you promised me not two minutes ago." She rose and snatched his cup from the table and headed toward the kitchen. "I certainly hope the SDPD can spare you long enough to attend your daughter's wedding."

"That's not fair, Tessie."

"Tell me about it. Life isn't fair, Mike. Haven't you learned that by now?" She shooed him toward the door, an angry edge to her voice. "Go on. Get out of here. You're needed elsewhere."

"I love you, Tessie. Can we talk about this later?"

Jamming her hands onto her hips, Tessa whirled around to face him. "I love you, too," she told him, letting the words slip out unbidden, "but sometimes—love just isn't enough. Now go."

Mike stared at her for a moment, started to say something but didn't, then headed for the door, slamming it behind him.

"I do love you, Mike Garrett!" Tessa shouted at the closed door. "I'll always love you, but I cannot take second place in your life."

ten

Christmas Day dawned bright, sunny, and beautiful, the perfect day for a Christmas wedding. Her little girl was getting married.

Tessa stared out her bedroom window, the bedroom she'd shared with Mike, wondering where he was, if he was safe, and if he'd make it to their daughter's wedding. She'd thought perhaps she'd see him when she'd spent Christmas Eve with Katie and Jim, but Katie said he'd called and told her he was working round the clock on that murder case and wouldn't be able to make it. *Just like him,* she thought as she turned away from the window. *Mike will never change.*

She stumbled through the day, pressing the lovely ivory lace dress she'd selected from Della's shop to wear as mother of the bride, gathering the things she'd need to take to the church for decorating the sanctuary, and doing a few mundane chores—but no matter how she tried, she couldn't get Mike off her mind.

About two o'clock, after loading everything in her car, Tessa headed for the church, determined not to let her lousy mood deter her from enjoying what should be one of the happiest days of her life.

After hanging her dress in the changing room, she went about her tasks placing the candles in the candelabra, attaching the big satin bows to the pews, unrolling the white plastic runner down the center aisle, placing the guest book in the foyer, and dozens of other things she'd told Katie she would do. Both the florist and caterer arrived at five. Tessa checked the final details with both then left them to their work while she tended to a few more unfinished chores. At last, everything was in readiness. Katie and the rest of the wedding party wouldn't begin to arrive for well over an hour.

Tessa stood back admiring the lovely, decorated sanctuary, the ivy-bedecked arch where Katie and Jim would repeat their vows, and the beauty of the flowers she and Mike had selected and the florist had so perfectly placed. Mike. What fun they'd had helping with Katie's wedding. She smiled to herself as she remembered how Mike had tried to save money by having the groomsmen wear their own shoes, and how he'd suggested they buy cookies at the deli and make punch from that tropical-type stuff for the reception. And how later he'd said he would do whatever was necessary to give his daughter the kind of wedding she deserved.

By working together, even the worst of situations had been handled and resolved, including the fiasco of the wrong wedding dress. *These are the kind of things we'll laugh about in years to come,* she told herself, smiling.

Then she sobered. "We?" she asked aloud. "Mike and me? There is no Mike and me!"

Tessa lowered herself onto one of the kneeling pads that graced the foot of the platform and, speaking aloud since she was alone in the church, called out to God. "God, am I being unreasonable? Is spending a few nights alone while Mike is off working worth giving up the time we have left to spend together? He'll be retiring in a few years and maybe then we would have time together, but what about now? I hate being alone. Why hasn't he been able to understand that? All I ever wanted was my husband by my side, not having to run off every time the telephone rang. Was that so wrong?"

She pulled a tissue from her purse and dabbed at her eyes.

"God, how can You love me when I'm so unlovable? How could Mike love me?"

Tears of repentance rolled down her cheeks. "I'm so sorry! Sorry for not trying to work out a compromise with Mike. . . For all the times I've complained about him to our daughter. . . For being so quick to judge him. . . For turning away from You when You didn't make Mike bend to my will. . . I'm a mess, a pitiful mess. All the things Mike has done on his job have counted. Because of his bravery and dedication, lives have been saved and perhaps hundreds of criminals have been placed behind bars."

She lowered her head, sobbing from a broken heart. "The works I've done for You are as filthy rags in comparison to his, especially since I did them all to seek the praise and favor of people. God, I know I have no right to ask You, but I beg You, forgive my hardened heart. Give me a spirit of forgiveness. Help me accept the fact that Mike didn't leave me because he wanted to. He left me to protect and serve the people of San Diego. He's asked me over and over to forgive him, but my foolish pride wouldn't allow it. I need that spirit of forgiveness. Help me to put aside the things that separated us. I—I don't want to lose whatever chance we may have to get back together. I love Mike dearly. I'll always love him."

❧

Mike stood at the back of the sanctuary, the garment bag containing his tuxedo held tightly in his hands, his insides aching as he listened to Tessa pour her heart out to God. Tears of remorse he was unable to control flowed down his tough-guy face. *Oh, Tessie, I love you, too! I don't want to lose you either!* Not sure what to do or if she would be offended that he'd been listening to her private conversation with God, he quietly draped the bag over a pew and crept slowly forward.

Lifting tear-filled eyes, Tessa stared at the huge stained glass window of Christ and the one lost sheep. "God—I'm like that little sheep. I've wandered so far away. I'm leaving this in Your hands. Melt me, God. Mold me into what You would have me to be. Only You can put back the miserable pieces of our lives."

Mike moved silently up beside her and knelt, slipping his arm about her. "Tessie—sweetheart," he whispered into her ear, "I spent most of yesterday with Pastor McIntosh. I've made my peace with God. I confessed my sins and asked Him to forgive me. Now I'm asking you to forgive me." His grip about her shoulders tightened. "No, I'm *begging* you to forgive me. We've let eight long years slip through our fingers, babe. Let's not waste what time we have left."

He waited, not sure if she was going to slap him, tell him to get lost, or a miracle would happen and she'd forgive him.

◆

Tessa's quickened heartbeat thundered in her ears. What did Mike say? That he'd made his peace with God? Oh, if only that were true! It had torn her apart watching him ignore God, the God that at one time he'd loved dearly and had taken great pleasure in serving.

"I'm a different man, Tessie. My priorities have changed. If you'll forgive me and give me another chance, I promise I won't let you down."

Her heart overflowing with love, Tessa reached up and cupped his face between her palms. "You have no idea how much I want to believe that, Mike."

"With God's help, dearest, I'll always be there for you. I don't want to face life without you."

Tessa stared into Mike's eyes and found love radiating there. True love. A love she could trust. Casting all her concerns aside, she slipped her arms about his strong neck, twisting the curls at the nape like she'd done so many times during their first years of marriage. "I can and will forgive you, Mike, but promise you'll forgive me, too. I've been a selfish, stupid fool."

Mike brushed a lock of hair from her forehead and kissed her cheek. "No, Tessie—I'm the one who has been a fool—a fool for putting our marriage in jeopardy by letting too many things come between us. I'm the one who needs to ask forgiveness."

Tessa leaned into him, pressing her cheek against his and nestling into the safety and security of his strong arms. "I love you so much, Mike."

"And I love you, babe. I can't begin to tell you how much."

Mike's cell phone rang, piercing the silence in the sanctuary. Instinctively, Tessa pulled away.

Mike pulled the phone from his belt. "Garrett."

He listened a moment then said, "No, not this time. I don't care how important it is, someone else will have to follow up on it. This is my day off. From now on, I'll be working only my regular hours. I'll be spending the rest of the time with my wife. Understood?"

Tessa couldn't believe what she was hearing. Mike actually refused to go when the SDPD called him? Amazing!

"I mean it, Tessie," he told her, holding her close and stroking her hair. "No more running every time the phone rings. I'll put in my shift and fill in if one of the guys is sick or his wife is in labor, but that's it. From now on you—if you'll let me share my life with you—you and the Lord are my number one priority. I want us to grow old together, enjoy our grandkids, and take care of one another in the sunset of our lives. I can't bear living without you, Tessie. Being with you these past two weeks, holding your hand, seeing your smile—well, I just know we belong together."

Tessa thought she would explode with happiness. Her dreams had come true. "I want that, too, Mike. I've never wanted anything but to be near you and be your wife in every way."

eleven

Mike stole a glance at the friends and relatives who had gathered for his daughter's wedding. His and Tessa's best friends, Bill and Ellen Zobel; their twin daughters Valene and her husband Jordan, Vanessa and her husband Nathan and their son, Jeff; Katie's friend Della and her husband Brandon; and so many others who had meant so much to them over the years. What a day this was. A real milestone in his and Tessa's life. One they'd never forget. Their baby girl was getting married.

He turned and lovingly smiled at Tessa where she sat on the front row of the beautiful, candlelit sanctuary holding his hand. In his eyes, Tessa had never looked lovelier, nor had he ever loved her more than at this moment.

"Who gives this woman to be married to this man?" Pastor McIntosh asked, looking toward them.

Mike lifted his chin high as he pulled Tessa to her feet. After wrapping an arm about her and pulling her close, in unison, they answered, "We do."

Beaming, Katie gave them an approving thumbs-up as the pair sat down.

"She's so lovely," Tessa whispered in Mike's ear. "How could we be so lucky?"

Mike leaned and planted a kiss on her cheek. "She looks exactly like you, babe."

Blushing, she gave him a smile that made his heart sing.

They listened attentively to every word the pastor said as he preached the sermon he'd spoken about at the rehearsal.

Finally, Pastor McIntosh turned to Katie and Jim. "It's time to pledge your love and your lives to one another. You may repeat your vows."

Katie, instead of turning to face Jim, whirled around and looked directly at Mike and Tessa. As if she was wondering what was going on, Tessa cast a quick glance toward Mike.

"Mom. Dad," Katie said, holding out her opened hand. "Would you please join Jim and me at the altar?"

Katie had called Mike to her dressing room just minutes before the wedding and told him she'd witnessed her parents' conversation in the sanctuary, and then filled him in on her idea. It was brilliant; he'd give her that. Mike couldn't keep a broad smile from traveling the full width of his face. Before Tessa could protest, he pulled her to her feet and up onto the platform.

"Mom, Daddy has something he wants to ask you," Katie said with a grin and a wink toward her father.

Mike dropped to one knee in front of Tessa then pulled a shiny gold band from his pocket and held it up for her to see. It was the very ring she had thrown at him the day she'd ordered him out of the house eight years ago—the ring he'd been carrying in his pocket for the last several days.

"Tessie, my precious, you're the only woman I've ever loved. Will you marry me? Again?"

A hush fell over the audience as Tessa stared into his face. Legally, she was still his wife. But Mike prayed, hoping she was as eager to renew their vows and let God help them start their marriage over as he was.

Suddenly she broke out into an adoring smile. "Mike," she said, touching his face with her fingertips, "of course I'll marry you, my love."

Mike had never been so happy. "How about now?" he

asked, holding out the ring again.

Tessa glanced toward the bride. "Katie?"

Katie nodded. "Nothing would make me happier than to see my parents together again."

Turning back to Mike, Tessa nodded. "Now would be wonderful!"

The audience broke into a loud applause as Mike and Tessa moved hand in hand to join Katie and Jim at the altar for another Christmas wedding.

epilogue

Three months later

Mr. and Mrs. Mike Garrett sat propped up in bed, leisurely reading the Saturday morning paper.

"I could take early retirement," Mike said, peeping over the top of the page.

Tessa tilted her head to one side and frowned. "And do what? Play golf? Maybe sit around the house all day wishing you were still working at the SDPD? I don't think so. Besides, we're still paying on Katie's wedding."

He folded the paper then moved closer and slipped an arm about her. "I'd do it, if it'd make you happy. We'd manage somehow."

She kissed his cheek then gently thumped his nose with the tip of her finger. "Now that you've informed the chief of police you'll no longer work on Sundays so we can attend church together, I'm totally happy."

He chucked her chin and gave her a teasing smile. "You're sure about that? It'll be nearly four years before I can retire and draw my full benefits."

She nodded. "I think I can wait that long. Now that you're spending so much time with me, I don't even mind the occasional calls you get from the SDPD wanting you to work on your days off."

She'd barely gotten the words out of her mouth when his cell phone rang.

"Garrett." He frowned as he listened.

The serious expression on his face told Tessa the call was urgent.

"Sorry. Gotta go, babe. They found another Jane Doe. I could be gone all day, maybe into the night. We've got to catch this guy before he strikes again. He's terrorized the women of San Diego far too long."

Tessa scooted off the bed and pulled on her robe. "I'll fix you a hot thermos of coffee."

Unable to resist another opportunity for a kiss, Mike grabbed her wrist and pulled her to him. "Sure you don't mind?"

She shook her head. "Not one bit. Just promise me you'll be careful. I'll be waiting for you, no matter how late it is." Standing on tiptoes, she planted a kiss on his lips. "Go get 'em, big guy."

A Letter To Our Readers

Dear Reader:

In order that we might better contribute to your reading enjoyment, we would appreciate your taking a few minutes to respond to the following questions. We welcome your comments and read each form and letter we receive. When completed, please return to the following:

Fiction Editor
Heartsong Presents
PO Box 719
Uhrichsville, Ohio 44683

1. Did you enjoy reading *Love Worth Keeping* by Joyce Livingston?
   ❏ Very much! I would like to see more books by this author!
   ❏ Moderately. I would have enjoyed it more if

   _____

   _____

   _____

2. Are you a member of **Heartsong Presents**? ❏ Yes ❏ No
   If no, where did you purchase this book? _____

   _____

3. How would you rate, on a scale from 1 (poor) to 5 (superior), the cover design? _____

4. On a scale from 1 (poor) to 10 (superior), please rate the following elements.

   ____ Heroine   ____ Plot
   ____ Hero   ____ Inspirational theme
   ____ Setting   ____ Secondary characters

5. These characters were special because? _____

_____

_____

6. How has this book inspired your life? _____

_____

_____

7. What settings would you like to see covered in future
Heartsong Presents books? _____

_____

_____

8. What are some inspirational themes you would like to see
treated in future books? _____

_____

_____

9. Would you be interested in reading other **Heartsong
Presents** titles? ❑ Yes ❑ No

10. Please check your age range:
    ❑ Under 18   ❑ 18-24
    ❑ 25-34   ❑ 35-45
    ❑ 46-55   ❑ Over 55

Name_____

Occupation _____

Address _____

City, State, Zip_____

Oregon Breeze

4 stories in 1

*F*eeling trapped by the way life has boxed them in, four Oregonians step out to embrace new challenges. Will a small step of faith free these lonely hearts to love completely? Or will circumstances bind them to the past?

Titles by author Birdie L. Etchison include: *Finding Courtney, The Sea Beckons, Ring of Hope,* and *Woodhaven Acres.*

Contemporary, paperback, 480 pages, 5³⁄₁₆" x 8"

Presents

Great Inspirational Romance at a Great Price!

Heartsong Presents books are inspirational romances in contemporary and historical settings, designed to give you an enjoyable, spirit-lifting reading experience. You can choose wonderfully written titles from some of today's best authors like Hannah Alexander, Andrea Boeshaar, Yvonne Lehman, Tracie Peterson, and many others.

When ordering quantities less than twelve, above titles are $2.97 each.
Not all titles may be available at time of order.

SEND TO: **Heartsong Presents** Reader's Service
P.O. Box 721, Uhrichsville, Ohio 44683
Please send me the items checked above. I am enclosing $ _____
(please add $2.00 to cover postage per order. OH add 7% tax. NJ
add 6%). Send check or money order, no cash or C.O.D.s, please.
To place a credit card order, call 1-740-922-7280.

NAME _____

ADDRESS _____

CITY/STATE _____ ZIP_____

HP 10-05